365 DAYS of WONDER

Mr. Browne's PRECEPTS

A QUOTE for EVERY DAY of the YEAR ABOUT COURAGE, FRIENDSHIP, LOVE, and KINDNESS

R.J. Palacio

ALFRED A. KNOPF
NEW YORK

THIS IS A BORZOI BOOK PUBLISHED BY ALFRED A. KNOPF

Copyright © 2014 by R. J. Palacio
Jacket art and interior illustrations copyright © 2016 by Vaughn Fender
All rights reserved. Published in the United States by Alfred A. Knopf,
an imprint of Random House Children's Books, a division of Penguin Random House
LLC, New York. Originally published in hardcover in slightly different form as
365 Days of Wonder: Mr. Browne's Book of Precepts by Alfred A. Knopf, an imprint of
Random House Children's Books, New York, in 2014.

Knopf, Borzoi Books, and the colophon are registered trademarks of
Penguin Random House LLC.

"Gracias a la Vida" copyright © 1966 by Violeta Parra

Visit us on the Web! randomhousekids.com
Educators and librarians, for a variety of teaching tools,
visit us at RHTeachersLibrarians.com

The Library of Congress has cataloged the hardcover edition of this work as follows:
Palacio, R. J.
365 Days of Wonder : Mr. Browne's Book of Precepts / R. J. Palacio.—First edition.
p. cm.
Summary: "A book of precepts, with one saying for each day,
from Auggie's teacher Mr. Browne." —Provided by publisher
ISBN 978-0-553-49904-9 (trade) — ISBN 978-0-553-49905-6 (lib. bdg.) —
ISBN 978-0-553-50903-8 (ebook)
1. Maxims. I. Title. II. Title: Mr. Browne's Book of Precepts.
PN6301.P27 2014
808.88'2 — dc23
2014009039
ISBN 978-0-399-55918-1 (pbk.)

Printed in the United States of America
August 2016
10
First Trade Paperback Edition
Random House Children's Books supports the First Amendment
and celebrates the right to read.

To Papi,
my first teacher

A teacher affects eternity;
he can never tell where his influence stops.

—Henry Adams

CONTENTS

Precepts or maxims are of great weight;

and a few useful ones at hand do more

toward a happy life than whole volumes

that we know not where to find.

—Seneca

My father's name was Thomas Browne. And *his* father's name was Thomas Browne. That's why *my* name is Thomas Browne. I didn't know until I was a college senior that there was a far more illustrious Thomas Browne, who had lived in England in the seventeenth century. Sir Thomas Browne was a gifted author, a student of the natural world, a scientist, a scholar, and an outspoken supporter of tolerance at a time when intolerance was the norm. In short, I couldn't have asked for a better namesake.

I started reading a lot of Sir Thomas Browne's works in college, including *Enquiries into Very many received Tenets, and commonly presumed Truths,* a book that set out to debunk the prevalent false beliefs of the day, and *Religio Medici,* a work that contained a number of religious inquiries that were considered highly unorthodox at the time. It was while reading the latter that I came across this wonderful line:

We carry within us the wonders we seek around us.

The beauty and power of that line stopped me cold, for some reason. Maybe it was exactly what I needed to hear at that particular moment in my life, a time when I was racked with indecision about whether the career I had chosen for myself—teaching—was full of enough "wonder" to keep me happy. I wrote the line down on a little slip of paper and taped it onto my wall, where it remained until I graduated. I took it with me to graduate school. I traveled with the Peace Corps and carried it in my wallet. My wife had it laminated and framed for me when we got married, and it now hangs in the foyer of our apartment in the Bronx.

It was the first of many precepts in my life, which I began collecting in a scrapbook. Lines from books I've read. Fortune cookies. Hallmark card homilies. I even wrote down the Nike ad line "Just do it!" because I thought it was the perfect directive for me. You can draw inspiration from anywhere, after all.

I first introduced precepts to my students as a student teacher. I was having a hard time getting my kids interested in the essay-writing unit—I believe I had asked them to write one hundred words on something that meant a lot to them—so I brought in the laminated Thomas Browne quote to show them something that meant a lot to me. Well, it turned out they were much more interested in exploring the meaning of the quote itself than they were in its impact on me, so I asked them to write about that instead. I was amazed at the things they came up with!

Ever since then, I've used precepts in my classroom. According to *Merriam-Webster,* a precept is "a command or principle intended especially as a general rule of action." For my students, I've always defined it in simpler terms: precepts are "words to live by." Easy. At the beginning of every month, I write a new precept on the board, they copy it, and then we discuss it. At the end of the month, they write an essay about the precept. Then at the end of the year, I give out my home address and ask the kids to send me a postcard over the summer with a new precept of their own, which could be a quote from a famous person or a precept they've made up. The first year I did this, I remember wondering if I'd get a single precept. I was floored when, by the end of summer, every single student in *each* of my classes had sent one in! You can imagine my further astonishment when, the following summer, the same thing happened again. Only this time, it wasn't only from my current class that I received postcards. I also got a handful from the previous year's class!

I've been teaching for ten years. As of this writing, I have about two thousand precepts. When Mr. Tushman, the middle-school director at Beecher Prep, heard this, he suggested that I collect them and turn them into a book that I could share with the world.

I was intrigued by the idea, for sure, but where to start? How to choose what precepts to include? I decided I would focus on themes with particular resonance for kids: kindness, strength of character, overcoming adversity, or simply doing good in the world. I like precepts that somehow elevate the soul. I chose one precept for every day of the year. My hope is that the reader of this book will begin every new day with one of these "words to live by."

I'm thrilled to be able to share my favorite precepts here. Many are ones I've collected myself over the years. Some were submitted by students. All mean a lot to me. As I hope they will to you.

—Mr. Browne

Teach him then the sayings of the past,

so that he may become a good example

for the children. . . . No one is born wise.

— The Maxims of Ptahhotep,
2200 BC

JANUARY

We carry within us the wonders we seek around us.

—Sir Thomas Browne

And above all, watch with glittering eyes the whole world around you because the greatest secrets are always hidden in the most unlikely places. Those who don't believe in magic will never find it.

—Roald Dahl

Three things in human
life are important:
the first is to be kind;
the second is to be
kind; and the third
is to be kind.

—Henry James

No man
is an
island,
entire
of itself.

—John Donne

I yam what
I yam.

—Popeye the Sailor (Elzie Crisler Segar)

All you need is love.

—John Lennon and
Paul McCartney

The two most
important days in
your life are the
day you are born
and the day you
find out why.

—Mark Twain

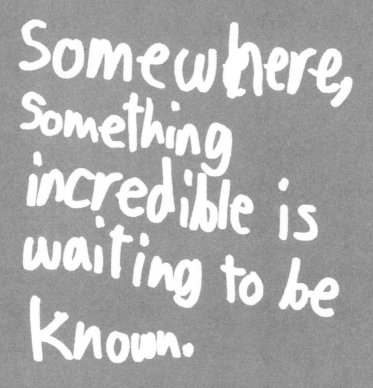

Somewhere, something incredible is waiting to be known.

—Carl Sagan

To be able to look
back upon one's life
in satisfaction, is to
live twice.

—Kahlil Gibran

If the wind will
not serve, take
to the oars.

—Latin proverb

Don't tell me
The Sky's the
Limit When there's
footprints On
The Moon.

—Paul Brandt

How wonderful it
is that nobody need
wait a single moment
before starting to
improve the world.

—Anne Frank

However long the night ... the dawn will break.

—African proverb

He who knows
others is clever,
but he who knows
himself is
enlightened.

—Lao Tzu

dreams come true is to wake up.

—Paul Valéry

Just be who
you want
to be,
not what
others
want to see.

—Unknown

NOT ALL THOSE WHO WANDER ARE LOST

—J.R.R. Tolkien

Make kindness your
daily modus operandi and
change your world.

—Annie Lennox

You are braver than you believe, stronger than you seem, and smarter than you think.

—Christopher Robin (A. A. Milne)

Have you
had a
kindness
shown?
Pass it on.

—Henry Burton

Don't dream it, be it.

—*The Rocky Horror Picture Show*

The miracle is not to fly in the air, or to walk on the water, but to walk on the earth.

—Chinese proverb

There is no shame in not knowing. The shame lies in not finding out.

—Assyrian proverb

To thine own self be true.

—William Shakespeare

No act of kindness, no matter how small, is ever wasted.

—Aesop

Be yourself,
Everyone Else is
already taken.

—Oscar Wilde

Wherever there is a human being there is an opportunity for a kindness.

—Seneca

Know thyself.

—Inscription at the Oracle of Delphi

Laughter is sunshine; it chases winter from the human face.

—Victor Hugo

The future belongs to those who believe in the beauty of their dreams.

—Eleanor Roosevelt

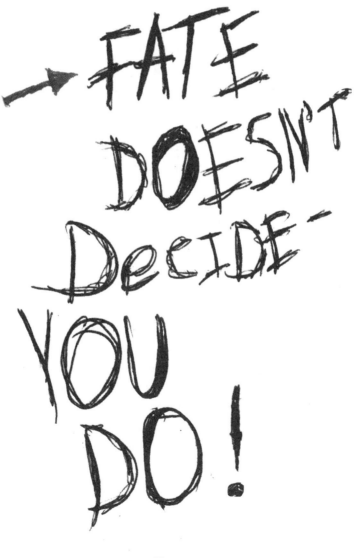

—Dominic

Here's a secret, kids: parents spend a lot of time teaching you how to be polite when you're very young because, it's a scientific fact, the world is nicer to polite people. *"Don't forget to say please,"* we tell you. *"Play nice. Say thank you."* These are elemental virtues. We teach them because they're good things to teach. And we want people to like you.

By the time you guys get to middle school, though, our priorities seem to shift. *"Do well in school. Succeed. Study harder. Have you finished your homework yet?"* That's what we tend to harp on then. Somewhere along the way, we stop emphasizing those elemental virtues. Maybe it's because we assume you've learned them by now. Or maybe it's because we've got so many other things we want you to learn. Or maybe, just maybe, it's because there's an unwritten law about middle-school kids: it's hard to be nice. The world may prefer polite children, but other middle schoolers don't seem to really appreciate them. And we parents, eager to see you guys get through these *Lord of the Flies* years, often turn a blind eye to some of the mean stuff that passes for normal.

I personally don't buy this notion that all kids go through a "mean phase." In fact, I think it's a lot of malarkey! Not to mention a little insulting to kids. When I talk to parents who tell me, as a way of justifying something unkind their child has done, "What can I do? Kids will be kids," it's all I can do not to bop them on their heads with a friendship bracelet.

Here's the thing: with all due respect, guys, I don't think you're always equipped to figure things out on your own. Sometimes there's a lot of unnecessary meanness that happens while you're trying to sort out who you want to be, who your friends are, who your friends are not. Adults spend a lot of time talking about bullying in schools these days, but the real problem isn't as obvious as one kid throwing a Slurpee in another kid's face. It's about social isolation. It's about cruel jokes. It's about the way kids treat one another. I've seen it with my own eyes, how old friends can turn against each other: it seems, sometimes, that it's not enough for them to go their separate ways—they literally have to "ice" their old buddies out just to prove to the new friends that they're no longer still friends. That's the kind of stuff I don't find acceptable. Fine, don't be friends anymore: but stay kind about it. Be respectful. Is that too much to ask?

Na-hah. I don't think so.

Every day at 3:10 p.m., my fifth graders stream out of Beecher Prep at dismissal time. A few of you, the ones who live nearby, walk home. Some of you take a bus or the subway. A lot of you, though, are picked up by parents or caregivers. The point is, either way, most parents don't allow their kids to roam around the city without knowing where they are, who they're with, and what they're doing. Why is that? Because you're still kids! So why should we let you roam wild in the uncharted territory of middle school without just a little bit of guidance? You're asked to navigate social situations every day—lunchroom politics, peer pressure, teacher relations. Some of you do it very well on your own, absolutely! But others—and let's be honest here—don't. Some of you still need a little help figuring things out.

So, kids, don't get mad at us if we try to help you in this regard. Be patient with us. It's always tricky, as a parent, striking the right balance between too much intervention and too little. So bear with us. We're only trying to help. When we remind you about those old, elemental virtues we used to teach you back in your toddler days, when you were still playing in sandboxes, it's because "playing nice" is something that doesn't end when you start middle school. It's something you need to remember every day as you walk through the school hallways on your way to becoming adults.

The truth of the matter is this: there's so much nobility lurking inside your souls. Our job as parents, and educators, and teachers, is to nurture it, to bring it out, and to let it shine.

—Mr. Browne

FEBRUARY

It is better
to ask
some of the
questions
than to know
all the
answers.

—James Thurber

I expect to pass through
this world but once.
Any good, therefore,
that I can do or any
kindness I can show
to any fellow creature,
let me do it now.
Let me not defer or
neglect it, for I
shall not pass this
way again.

—Stephen Grellet

The supreme happiness
of life is the conviction
that we are loved.

—Victor Hugo

L♥ve
a little
more
each day.

—Madison

Give me a firm
place to stand,
and I will move
the earth.

—Archimedes

I am an
expression
of the
divine.

—Alice Walker

If you ever
feel lost,

let your

heart

be your compass.

—Emily

Everything
you can
imagine
is real.

—Pablo Picasso

If thou follow
thy star, thou
canst not fail of
glorious haven.

—Dante Alighieri

Find Your GREATNESS

—Rebecca

We all have the same roots, and we are all branches of the same tree.

—Aang (*Avatar: The Last Airbender*)

Man can learn
nothing unless he
proceeds from
the known to the
unknown.

—Claude Bernard

—Lindsay

To be loved, be lovable.

—Ovid

The smile is the
shortest
distance between
two persons.

—Victor Borge

Those who try to do something and Fail are infinitely better than those who try to do nothing and succeed.

—Lloyd Jones

FEBRUARY 17

—Jack

The main thing is
to be moved, to love,
to hope, to tremble,
to live.

—Auguste Rodin

The greatest
glory in living
lies not in
never falling,
but in rising
every time
we fall.

—Nelson Mandela

Whatever you are, be a good one.

—Abraham Lincoln

Don't tell me
not to fly, I've
simply got to.

—Bob Merrill and Jule Styne,
"Don't Rain on My Parade"

Kindly words
do not enter
so deeply into
men as a
reputation
for kindness.

—Mencius

Hard work
beats talent
when talent
doesn't work
hard ☺

—Shreya

Keep a green tree in your heart
and a singing bird may come.

—Chinese proverb

They are
never alone
that are
accompanied
with noble
thoughts.

—Sir Philip Sidney

When you come to the
end of your rope, tie a
knot in it and hang on.

—Thomas Jefferson

It's not what
happens to you,
but how you react
that matters.

—Epictetus

For
kindness
begets
kindness
evermore.

—Sophocles

FEBRUARY 29

BE NICE TO EACH OTHER IT'S REALLY ALL THAT MATTERS.

—Dawn Lafferty Hochsprung
SANDY HOOK ELEMENTARY SCHOOL

I like including a precept about discovery at this time of year. Why this time of year? Because, although February is the shortest month, it also happens to be the longest stretch of time without an event to look forward to (Presidents' Day notwithstanding). In January, students have just come off the holiday high that is December. With the rush of presents and the thrill of the first few snowfalls behind them, by January 31 the realization hits: "We won't have another big stretch of vacation time until spring break!" Argh! Hence: the February doldrums.

I've always found that it helps to get my students thinking about unexplored frontiers—be they frontiers of the imagination or geographical frontiers. The latter dovetail nicely with what they're usually doing in history at this time of year (exploring either ancient China or ancient Greece, depending on their history teacher), and the former are a great segue into my Creative Writing unit.

I recently used the James Thurber precept "It is better to ask some of the questions than to know all the answers" and got a really interesting essay back from a student named Jack Will.

> I like this precept a lot a lot a lot. It makes me think about all the stuff I don't know. And maybe never, ever will know. I spend a lot of time asking myself questions. Some are stupid questions. Like, why does poop smell so bad? Why don't human beings come in as many shapes and sizes as dog breeds do?

(I mean, a mastiff is like ten times bigger than a Chihuahua, so why aren't there humans who are sixty feet tall?) But I also ask myself bigger questions. Like, why do people have to die? Why can't we just print more money and give it to people who don't have enough of it? Stuff like that.

So, the big question I've been asking myself a lot this year is, why do we all look the way we do? Why do I have one friend who looks "normal" and another friend who doesn't? These are the kinds of questions that I don't think I'll ever know the answers to. But asking myself the questions did make me ask myself another question, which is, what is "normal" anyway?

So I looked it up in oxforddictionaries.com. This is what it said:

normal (adjective): Conforming to a standard; usual, typical, or expected.

And I was like, "conforming to a standard"? "Usual? Typical? Expected?" Ugh! Who the heck wants to be "expected" anyway? How lame is that?

So that's why I really like this precept.

Because it's true! It's better to ask some really awesome questions than it is to know a lot of dumb answers to stupid stuff. Like, who cares what x equals in some dumb equation? Duh! Answers like that don't matter! But the question "What is normal?" does matter! It matters because there's never going to be a right answer. And there's no wrong answer, either. The question is all that matters!

This is why I love using precepts in my classroom. You throw them out there, and you never know what you're getting back, what's going to strike a chord with a kid, or what's going to make them think a little deeper, a little bigger, than if they were just trying to answer a question from a book. It's one of the things I love most about precepts: the sentiments they voice are usually about things that human beings have been grappling with since the dawn of time. I love that my fifth graders are doing the same!

—Mr. Browne

MARCH

Kind words do not cost much. Yet they accomplish much.

—Blaise Pascal

Never doubt that
a small group of
thoughtful, committed
citizens can change
the world.
Indeed, it's the
only thing that ever has.

—Margaret Mead

To me, every hour of

the light and dark

is a miracle,

Every inch

of space is a miracle.

—Walt Whitman

How like an Angel came I down!

—Thomas Traherne

Superheroes are made but heroes are born.

—Antonio

A tree is known by its
fruit; a man by his deeds.
A good deed is never lost;
he who sows courtesy
reaps friendship, and
he who plants kindness
gathers love.

—St. Basil

Do not go where
the path may
lead, go instead
where there is no
path and leave
a trail.

—Ralph Waldo Emerson

Life is a ticket to
the greatest show
on earth.

—Martin H. Fischer

To know what
you know and
what you do not
know, that is
true knowledge.

—Confucius

Happiness is not something ready-made. It comes from your own actions.

—Dalai Lama

Always do right. This will
gratify some people and
astonish the rest.

—Mark Twain

That Love is all there is,
Is all we know of Love.

—Emily Dickinson

What lies behind us
and what lies before
us are but tiny matters
compared to what lies
within us.

—Henry Stanley Haskins

Thousands of candles can be lit from a single candle, and the life of the single candle will not be shortened. Happiness never decreases by being shared.

—Bukkyo Dendo Kyokai,
The Teaching of Buddha

Paradise on Earth is where I am.

—Voltaire

In this world, one needs
to be a little too good in order
to be good enough.

—Pierre Carlet de Chamblain de Marivaux

Good actions are the
invisible hinges on the
doors of heaven.

—Victor Hugo

Be the person
who can smile
on the
worst day.

—Cate

Don't just go
with the flow,
take some
dares through
the rapids.

—Isabelle

Where there is love, there is joy.

—Mother Teresa

Hope is like THE Sun. When it's behind the clouds, it's not gone, you just have to FIND it!

—Matthew

your
best
takes
your
time.

—Thomas

What wisdom can you find that is greater than kindness?

—Jean-Jacques Rousseau

The man who moves a
mountain must start by
moving small stones.

—Chinese proverb

You can do anything you want. All you have to do is

Believe

—Ella

Be kind whenever
possible. It is always
possible.

—Dalai Lama

As soon as you trust yourself,
you will know how to live.

—Johann Wolfgang von Goethe

We must dare,
dare again,
and go on
daring!

——Georges Jacques Danton

No bird soars too high if he
soars with his own wings.

—William Blake

Life is about using the whole box of crayons.

—RuPaul

Life is
like a
rollercoaster...

...with all its ups and downs.

—Kyler

When Tommy, my son, was three years old, my wife, Lilly, and I took him for his annual checkup and the pediatrician asked us what his eating habits were like.

"Well," we confessed, "he's going through this phase of only liking chicken fingers and carbs, so we've kind of given up trying to get him to eat vegetables for now. It's become too much of a struggle every night."

The pediatrician nodded and smiled, and then said, "Well, you can't really force him to eat the veggies, guys, but your job is to make sure they're on his plate. He can't eat them if they're not even on his plate."

I've thought about that a lot over the years. I think about it with teaching. My students can't learn what I don't teach them. Kindness. Empathy. Compassion. It's not part of the curriculum, I know, but I still have to keep dishing it out onto their plates every day. Maybe they'll eat it; maybe they won't. Either way, my job is to keep on serving it to them. Hopefully, a little mouthful of kindness today may make them hungry for a bigger taste of it tomorrow.

—Mr. Browne

What is beautiful is good, and who is good will soon be beautiful.

—Sappho

'Tis always
morning
somewhere in
the world.

—Richard Henry Hengist Horne

Knowledge, in truth, is the
great sun in the firmament.
Life and power are scattered
with all its beams.

—Daniel Webster

Nothing can make our life, or the lives of other people, more beautiful than perpetual kindness.

—Leo Tolstoy

—Delaney

Be the change
you want to see
in the world.

—Mahatma Gandhi

Life can only be understood
backwards; but it must be
lived forwards.

—Søren Kierkegaard

Heaven is under our feet as well as over our heads.

—Henry David Thoreau

Be noble! and the nobleness that lies
In other men, sleeping but never dead,
Will rise in majesty to meet thine own.

—James Russell Lowell

He was a bold man that first ate an oyster.

—Jonathan Swift

It's not whether
you get knocked down,
it's whether you get up.

—Vince Lombardi

The world is good-natured
to people who are
good-natured.

—William Makepeace Thackeray

The
universe
is what
you
illustrate
it to be.

—Rory

The difference
between ordinary
and extraordinary
is that little extra.

—Jimmy Johnson

I am only one,

But still I am one.

I cannot do everything,

But still I can do something;

And because I cannot do everything,

I will not refuse to do the something that I can do.

—Edward Everett Hale

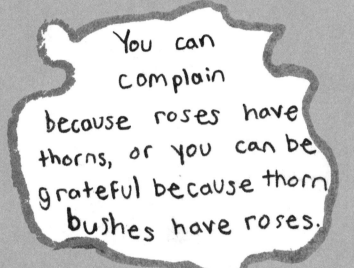

—Ziggy (Tom Wilson)

Use what talent
you possess: the
woods would be very
silent if no birds
sang except those
that sang best.

——Henry van Dyke

The goal of life is to make
your heartbeat match the
beat of the universe, to match
your nature with Nature.

—Joseph Campbell

Even the
toughest
Dogs can
be afraid
of vacuums.

—Anna

Do a deed of
simple kindness;
though its end
you may not see,
it may reach, like
widening
ripples, down a
long eternity.

—Joseph Norris

We love the things we love for what they are.

—Robert Frost

Ideals are like stars; you will not succeed in touching them with your hands. But like the seafaring man on the desert of waters, you choose them as your guides, and following them you will reach your destiny.

—Carl Schurz

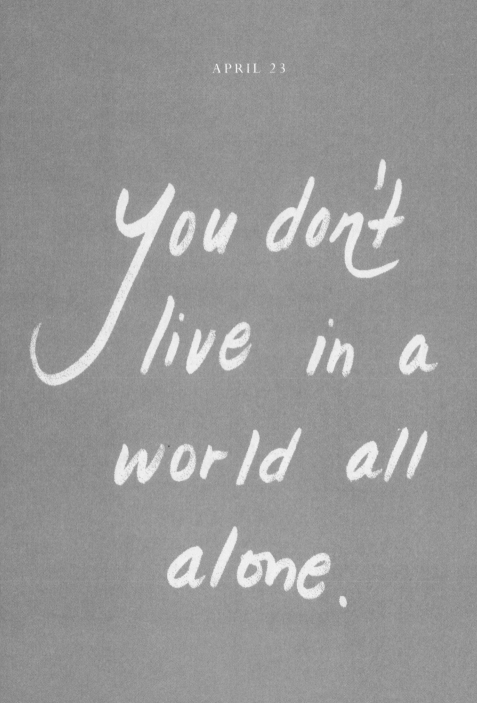

You don't live in a world all alone.

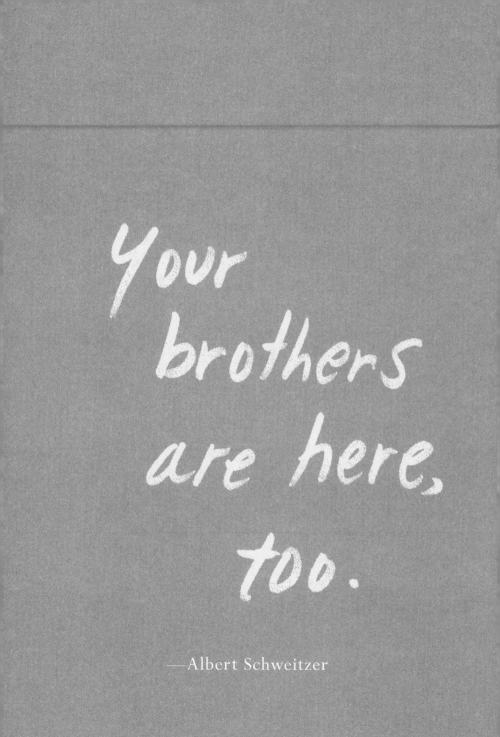

Your brothers are here, too.

—Albert Schweitzer

I feel no need for
any other faith than my faith
in human things.

—Pearl S. Buck

Today I have grown
taller from walking
with the trees.

—Karle Wilson Baker

The great man does not think
beforehand of his words that they
may be sincere, nor of his actions
that they may be resolute—he simply
speaks and does what is right.

—Mencius

Wherever you are it is your own friends who make your world.

—William James

There are
many great
deeds
done in
the small
struggles
of life.

—Victor Hugo

Don't wait until you know
who you are to get started.

—Austin Kleon

To each, his own is
beautiful.

—Latin proverb

My grandparents were avid Scrabble players. They played every night, whether they had company or not—on the same Scrabble board they'd had for over fifty years. Their matches were formidable because they were both incredible players. Interestingly, my grandfather, who was known in my family as being the "intellectual," almost always lost to my grandmother. It's not that Grandma wasn't every bit as smart as Grandpa, by the way—it's just that he was the one who had gotten a degree at Columbia while Grandma stayed home to raise my mother and her sisters. Grandpa was a lawyer, and Grandma was a homemaker. Grandpa had a library of books, and Grandma liked doing crosswords. Grandpa hated to lose, and Grandma whipped his butt nine out of every ten games for over fifty years.

One time I asked Grandma what her secret to winning was, and she said, "It's simple. Just play your tiles."

"Okay, Grandma, a little elaboration is needed here," I answered.

"Here's why I always beat your grandfather. He hoards his tiles. When he gets good letters, he holds on to them, waiting to play on a triple-word score. He'll skip a turn to try and get a seven-letter word to get the fifty-point bonus. Or he'll trade in his letters in the hope he'll get better ones. That's no way to play!"

"It's his strategy," I said, trying to defend him.

She waved her hand in the air dismissively. "Me, I just play my tiles—whatever tiles I get. Doesn't matter if they're good letters or bad letters. Doesn't matter if they're on a triple-word score or not. Whatever tiles I get, I play. I make the most of them. That's why I always beat your grandpa."

"Does he know this?" I asked. "Haven't you ever shared this secret with him?"

"What secret? He's watched me play every night for fifty years—do you think my way of playing is a secret? Play the tiles you get! That's my secret."

"Grandpa," I said later to my grandfather. "Grandma told me the reason she always beats you at Scrabble is because she always plays her tiles and you hold on to yours. Have you ever thought about changing your style of playing a bit? Maybe you would win more often!"

Grandpa poked his finger into my chest. "That's the difference between your grandma and me," he answered. "I want to win, but only if I can win beautifully. Big, long words. Words no one's ever heard of before. That's me. Your grandmother, she's fine winning with nothing but a string of A's and O's. You know the old saying: *Suum cuique pulchrum est!* To each, his own is beautiful."

"That may be true, Grandpa, but Grandma's kicking your butt!" I said.

Grandpa laughed. *"Suum cuique pulchrum est!"*

—Mr. Browne

MAY

Play the tiles you get.

—Grandma Nelly

Do all the good you can,

By all the means you can,

In all the ways you can,

In all the places you can,

At all the times you can,

To all the people you can,

As long as you ever can.

—John Wesley

There is nothing
stronger in the world
than gentleness.

—Han Suyin

A single act of kindness throws out roots in all directions, and the roots spring up and make new trees.

—Father Faber

Winners never quit and quitters never win

—Vince Lombardi

Cherish that which is
within you.

—Chuang Tzu

Follow your dreams.
It may be a long
journey, but the
path is right in
front of you.

—Grace

It's not the load that
breaks you down.
It's the way you carry it.

—*C. S. Lewis*

Though we travel the world over to find the beautiful, we must carry it with us or we find it not.

—Ralph Waldo Emerson

The breeze at dawn has
secrets to tell you.
Don't go back to sleep.

—Rumi

IF PLAN "A" DOESN'T WORK, JUST REMEMBER: THE ALPHABET HAS 25 MORE LETTERS.

—Unknown

The world does not
know how much it
owes to the common
kindnesses which so
abound everywhere.

—J. R. Miller, *The Beauty of Kindness*

The best and most
beautiful things in
the world cannot be seen
or even touched.
They must be felt with
the heart.

—Helen Keller

You were
born An

Original.

don't

become

a copy.

—Dustin

FIND THINGS THAT SHINE AND MOVE TOWARD THEM.

—Mia Farrow

If you want to be
well-liked, you got
to be yourself.

—Gavin

If your
ship doesn't
come in,
swim out
to it.

—Jonathan Winters

All we are saying is give
peace a chance.

—John Lennon

The purpose of life is a
life of purpose.

—Robert Byrne

Believe in life!

—W.E.B. Du Bois

You're free to make your own choices, but you will never be free of the CONSEQUENCES of your choices.

—Srishti

Making a million friends is not a miracle . . . the miracle is to make such a friend who can stand with you when millions are against you.

—Unknown

Have I done an unselfish thing?
Well then, I have my reward.

—Marcus Aurelius

The wind is blowing.
Adore the wind!

—Pythagoras

The chief
happiness
for a man
is to be
what he is.

—Desiderius Erasmus

A single conversation
across the table with a wise
man is worth a month's
study of books.

—Chinese proverb

Your actions are all
you can own.

—Flynn

Just love life
and it will love
you back

—Madeline

Kindness is a
language the
deaf can hear
and the blind
can see.

—Mark Twain

Is it so small a thing
To have enjoyed the sun,
To have lived light
in the spring,
To have loved, to have
thought, to have done;
To have advanced true
friends, and beat
down baffling foes?

—Matthew Arnold

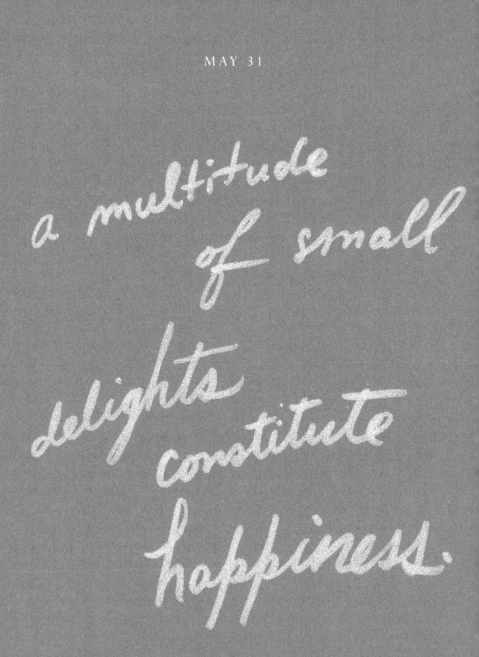

a multitude of small delights constitute happiness.

—Charles Baudelaire

Every now and again I have to remind my students that they're not invisible. "I can see you rolling your eyes!" I tell them. They think this is funny—usually. And it is—usually. But the other night I was reminded of how easy it is for kids to forget that their actions are, indeed, noted.

I was attending the upper-school play at Beecher Prep and took a seat next to the mother of one of my former students, whom I'll call Briana. This was a sweet, bright girl who had experienced some difficulties with a group of mean girls in middle school. Briana was shy and a little awkward, so I was surprised when her mom told me that she'd been cast in the lead role of the play. Her mom was so proud! She said that her daughter had really come out of her shell in upper school, due largely to the recognition she'd gotten for her singing and acting talent.

When the play started, the moment Briana came onstage, I understood what her mom meant. Gone was that awkward little girl I remembered from fifth grade, replaced by a very confident leading lady who could easily have been mistaken for a young Nicole Kidman. "Good for you, Briana!" I thought to myself. But no sooner had she finished singing her first verse than I noticed, sitting a couple of rows in front of us, those same three girls who used to taunt her in middle school. None of them even went to the school anymore (they hadn't been accepted to the upper school largely because of the school's strong anti-bullying commitment). These girls snickered the moment Briana came onstage. They whispered to one another behind open hands. I'm sure they didn't think anyone was noticing them, but I could see out of the corner of my eye that Briana's mom saw everything as clearly as I did. I can't even describe the look on her face. It was heartbreaking.

I waited for Briana to finish her solo. The moment the applause started, I leaned over the seat in front of me and tapped the shoulder of one of the girls. She turned around and started to smile when she saw me, but then she noticed my expression as I mouthed the words *Shut up!* The other girls saw this, too.

I think the shock of seeing Mr. Browne, their formerly mellow English teacher, so angry, using language that he had never used with them before, had its intended effect: they were quiet as church mice for the rest of the first act. During intermission, they quickly disappeared and didn't come back for Act Two.

By the time the play ended, I had almost forgotten about those idiotic girls amid the thunderous applause. I turned to Briana's mom to congratulate her on her daughter's truly brilliant performance. She was smiling, but there were tears in her eyes. I don't know if they were tears of pride or if there was a trace of bitterness over the fact that those girls had marred what should have been a completely joyful night for her. All I know is that my memory of those girls will be forever altered by their thoughtless behavior that night. I'm sure they didn't mean for Briana's mom to see them, but it doesn't matter. Your actions are noted, kids. And remembered.

—Mr. Browne

JUNE

Just follow the day and reach for the sun!

—The Polyphonic Spree

Ignorance is not
saying, I don't know.
Ignorance is saying,
I don't want to know.

—Unknown

Start by doing
the necessary,
then the possible,
and suddenly
you are doing
the impossible.

—St. Francis of Assisi

Don't worry about a thing
'cause every little thing is
gonna be all right.

—Bob Marley

A bit of fragrance clings to the hand
that gives flowers.

—Chinese proverb

Follow every
rainbow,
Till you find
your dream.

—Rodgers and Hammerstein

Life moves forward. If you keep looking back, you won't be able to see where you're going.

—Charles Carroll

The only person
you are destined to
become is the person
you decide to be.

—Ralph Waldo Emerson

One of the secrets of life is that all that is really worth the doing is what we do for others.

—Lewis Carroll

Whether you believe you can or believe you can't, you are absolutely right.

—Henry Ford

Fall seven times.
Stand up eight.

—Japanese proverb

The most beautiful thing
we can experience is
the mysterious. It is the
source of all true art
and science.

—Albert Einstein

Be humble, for you are
made of earth.
Be noble, for you are
made of stars.

—Serbian proverb

In a gentle
way, you can
shake the
world.

—Mahatma Gandhi

We do not ask for what useful
purpose the birds do sing, for
song is their pleasure
since they were created for
singing. Similarly, we ought
not to ask why the human
mind troubles to fathom the
secrets of the heavens. . . .

—Johannes Kepler

Your life is your story, go write it.

—Clare

Even if you don't win, listen to the small voice inside of you that says you are always a winner.

—Josh

When we know how to read our own hearts, we acquire wisdom of the hearts of others.

—Denis Diderot

Let me not
pray to be
sheltered from
dangers but to
be fearless in
facing them.

—Rabindranath Tagore

Thank you to life that has
given me so much.
It's given me the strength
of my weary feet,
With which I have walked
through cities and puddles,
Beaches and deserts,
Mountains and plains. . . .

—Violeta Parra, "Gracias a la Vida"

The greatest danger for
most of us is not that our
aim is too high and we
miss it, but that it is too
low and we reach it.

—Michelangelo Buonarroti

He who
travels has
stories to
tell.

—Gaelic proverb

Courage is found in
unlikely places.

—J.R.R. Tolkien

Every day, in every way, I'm getting better and better.

—Émile Coué

Sail the ocean
even when others stay
on the shore.

—Emma

LIFE IS NOT COLORFUL.

LIFE IS

COLORING

—Paco

The true secret of
happiness lies in taking
a genuine interest in all
the details of daily life.

—William Morris

How many things are looked upon as quite impossible until they have actually been effected?

—Pliny the Elder

Kindness is
like snow.
It beautifies
everything
it covers.

—Kahlil Gibran

Every day
may not
be glorious,
but there's something
glorious in
every day.

Find the glory!

—Caleb

I have to admit, I love getting postcard precepts in the summer. Some of them come on real postcards. Others come as part of longer letters, like this one:

> Dear Mr. Browne,
>   Here's my precept: "If you can get through middle school without hurting anyone's feelings, that's really cool beans."
>   I hope you are having a super-nice summer! My mom and I went to visit Auggie's family in Montauk on July 4th! They had fireworks on the beach! PLUS—there was a telescope on his roof! Every night I got to go up and look at the stars! Did I ever tell you that I want to be an astronomer when I grow up? I know all the constellations by heart. I also know a lot about the science of stars. For instance, do you know what stars are made of? Maybe you do because you're a teacher, but a lot of people don't. A star is pretty much just a giant cloud of hydrogen and helium gases. When it gets old, it starts to shrink, which kind of creates all these other elements. And then when all the elements get so tiny they can't go anywhere, they explode and send all their stardust into the universe! *That* dust is what forms planets and moons and mountains—and even people! Isn't that so awesome? We're all made of stardust!
>
>   Love,
>   Summer Dawson

Yep, I sure do love my job. As long as little kids like Summer keep reaching for the stars, I'll be here to cheer them on.

                                        —Mr. Browne

JUZY

Practice random kindness and senseless acts of beauty.

—Anne Herbert

Don't be afraid to take a
big step. You can't cross a
chasm in two small jumps.

—David Lloyd George

It is always easier to
fight for one's principles
than to live up to them.

—Alfred Adler

Great works are performed
not by strength but by
perseverance.

—Samuel Johnson

Shoot for the moon, because
even if you miss, you'll land
among the stars.

—Les Brown

Life is not
measured by
the number
of breaths we
take, but by
the moments
that take our
breath away.

—Unknown

Greatness lies not in being
strong, but in the right using
of strength.

—Henry Ward Beecher

Shall we make a new rule
of life from tonight: always to
try to be a little kinder than
is necessary?

—J. M. Barrie

—Buddha

There's only one corner
of the universe you can be
certain of improving, and
that's your own self.

—Aldous Huxley

At the end of the game,
pawns and kings go back
into the same box.

—Italian proverb

To the world,
You are one person.
But to one person,
You may be the

WORLD!

—Unknown

Each of us has his own alphabet with which to create poetry.

—Irving Stone

If something stands
to be gained, nothing
will be lost.

—Miguel de Cervantes

Determination is
the wake-up call
to the human will.

—Anthony Robbins

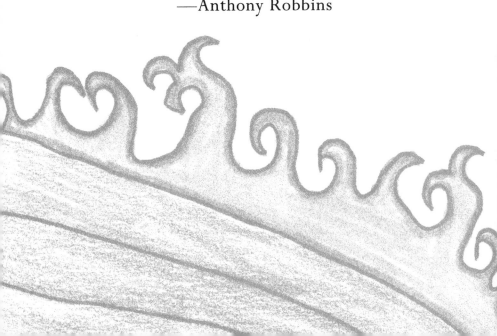

The sun'll come out

tomorrow.

—*Annie* (Martin Charnin)

Ride on! Rough-shod
if need be, smooth-shod if
that will do, but ride on!
Ride on over all obstacles,
and win the race!

—Charles Dickens

The best things in life are not things.

—Ginny Moore

Tomorrow to
fresh woods, and
pastures new.

—John Milton

If you want
to learn about
the world
go out in it.

—Mae

You miss
100 percent
of the shots
you don't take.

—Wayne Gretzky

Remember there's
no such thing as a
small act of kindness.
Every act creates a ripple
with no logical end.

—Scott Adams

SUCCESS

does not come through grades, degrees or distinctions. It comes through experiences that expand your belief in what is

POSSIBLE

—Matea

Believe you
can and
you're halfway
there.

—Theodore Roosevelt

An age is called Dark not
because the light fails to
shine but because people
fail to see it.

—James Michener

There is no wealth but life.

—John Ruskin

You're never
a loser until
you quit trying.

—Mike Ditka

Return to old watering
holes for more than
water; friends and dreams
are there to meet you.

—African proverb

The beauty of a living thing
is not the atoms that go
into it, but the way those
atoms are put together.

—Carl Sagan

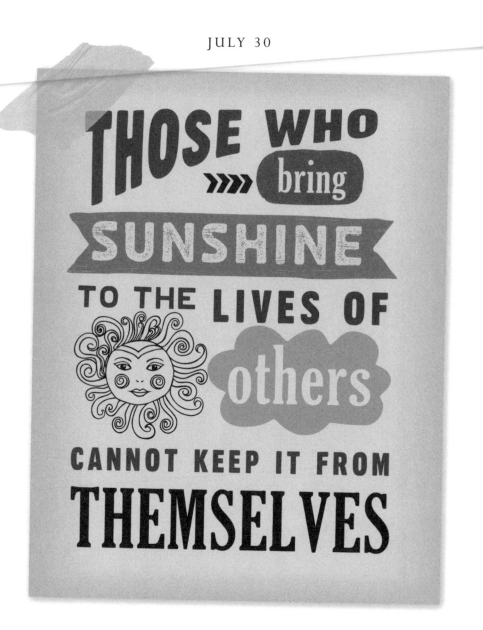

THOSE WHO >>> bring SUNSHINE TO THE LIVES OF others CANNOT KEEP IT FROM THEMSELVES

—J. M. Barrie

We must be willing
to let go of the life
we have planned, so
as to have the life
that is waiting for us.

—E. M. Forster

Sometimes people surprise you. You think you have them figured out, but they'll do something that makes you realize just how fathomless the human heart truly is. To that end, and because the heart of a child is still such a work in progress, no one can surprise you more than a child. This happened to me over the course of a recent email exchange with a former student. This kid did not have a great year in fifth grade. Most of it was his own doing: he made bad choices. He was something of a bully, and the tide turned against him, as it should have. He found that his small-minded dislikes weren't as universal as he thought, and that he was alone in his prejudices.

However, I always suspected that there was a little bit more to this boy than that. His personal essays betrayed a more feeling heart than his actions implied. At times, it was hard to reconcile the boy who could be so hateful with the boy who wrote the essays. So I held out hope for him. And when I got an email from him over the summer, I couldn't have been happier.

To: tbrowne@beecherschool.edu
Fr: julianalbans@ezmail.com
Re: My precept

Hi, Mr. Browne! I just sent you my precept in the mail: "SOMETIMES IT'S GOOD TO START OVER." It's on a postcard of a gargoyle. I wrote this precept because I'm going to a new school in September. I ended up hating Beecher Prep. I didn't like the students. But I DID like the teachers. I thought your class was great. So don't take my not going back personally.

I don't know if you know the whole long story, but basically the reason I'm not going back to Beecher Prep is . . . well, not to name names, but there was one student I really didn't get along with. Actually, it was two students. (You can probably guess who they are.) Anyway, these kids were not my favorite people in the world. We started writing mean notes to each other. I repeat: *each other*. It was a 2-way street! But I'm the one who got in trouble for it! Just me! It was so unfair! The truth is, Mr. Tushman had it in for me because my mom was trying to get him fired. Anyway, long story short: I got suspended for two weeks for writing the notes! (No one knows this, though. It's a secret, so please don't tell anyone.) The school said it had a "zero tolerance" policy against bullying. But I don't think what I did was bullying! My parents got so mad at the school! They decided to enroll me in a different school next year. So, yeah, that's the story.

I really wish that "student" had never come to Beecher Prep! My whole year would have been so much better! I hated having to be in his classes. He gave me nightmares. I would still be going to Beecher Prep if he hadn't been there. It's a bummer.

I really liked your class, though. You were a
great teacher. I wanted you to know that.

To: julianalbans@ezmail.com
Fr: tbrowne@beecherschool.edu
Re: Re: My precept

Hi, Julian. Thanks so much for your email! I'm
looking forward to getting the gargoyle postcard.
I was sorry to hear you won't be coming back
to Beecher Prep. I always thought you were a
great student and a gifted writer.

By the way, I love your precept. I agree,
sometimes it's good to start over. A fresh start
gives us the chance to reflect on the past, weigh
the things we've done, and apply what we've
learned from those things to the way we move
forward. If we don't examine the past, we don't
learn from it.

As for the "kids" you didn't like, I do think
I know who you're talking about. I'm sorry
the year didn't turn out to be a happy one for
you, but I hope you take a little time to ask
yourself why. Things that happen to us, even
the bad stuff, can often teach us a little bit
about ourselves. Do you ever wonder why you
had such a hard time with these two students?
Was it, perhaps, their friendship that bothered
you? Were you troubled by Auggie's physical
appearance? You mentioned that you started
having nightmares. Sometimes fear can make
even the nicest kids say and do things they

wouldn't ordinarily say or do. Perhaps you should explore these feelings further?

In any case, I wish you the best of luck in your new school, Julian. You're a good kid. A natural leader. Just remember to use your leadership for good, huh? Don't forget: always choose kind!

To: tbrowne@beecherschool.edu
Fr: julianalbans@ezmail.com
Re: Re: Re: My precept

Thanks so much for your email, Mr. Browne! It really made me feel good! Like, you really "get" me. And you don't think I'm a bad kid, which is nice. I feel like everyone thinks I'm this "demon child." It's nice to know you don't.

I had begun to read your email and my grandmother saw me smiling so she asked me to read it aloud to her. Grandmère is French. I'm staying with her in Paris for the summer. So I read it to her. And we got into this whole long talk after. Grandmère's old, but she's still kind of with it. And anyway, guess what? She totally agreed with you! She thinks maybe I was kind of mean to Auggie because I was a little afraid of him. And after talking to her about it, I think maybe you guys are right. The thing about the nightmares I was having is that I used to get bad nightmares when I was little. Night terrors. Anyway, I hadn't had one in a long time, but the first time I saw Auggie in Mr. Tushman's office,

I started having them again. It sucked! It actually made me not want to go to school because I didn't want to see his face again!

I know I would have had a better year if Auggie had never come to Beecher Prep. But I know it's not his fault that he looks the way he does. My grandmother told me this long story about a boy she knew when she was a girl, and how kids used to be mean to him. It made me feel so sorry for him! It made me feel bad about some of the things I said to Auggie.

So anyway, I wrote Auggie a note. I don't have his address, though, so can I mail it to you so that you could mail it to Auggie? I don't know how much the stamp costs, but I'll totally pay you back. (It's a nice note, btw! Don't worry!)

Thanks again, Mr. Browne. Seriously. Thanks!

To: julianalbans@ezmail.com
Fr: tbrowne@beecherschool.edu
Re: Proud!

Julian, I can't tell you how proud I am that you've taken this big step! I would be honored to mail that note to Auggie for you when I get it (and you don't have to worry about paying me back for the stamp). Looks like you're really living up to your precept. Good for you, Julian!

Look, the truth is, it's not easy coping with fear. In fact, it's one of the hardest things human beings have to face. That's because fear isn't always rational. Do you know the origin of fear? It goes back to the dawn of mankind. When we were pre-humans, we developed fear as a mechanism to survive in a tough world— poisonous snakes and spiders, saber-toothed cats, wolves. The instinctual response to a perceived danger would trigger adrenaline inside us, and we could run away faster, or fight better, in response to that perceived danger. It's a very natural instinct, Julian. To be afraid is one of the things that make us human.

But another thing that makes us human is our ability to deal with fear. We have other traits that we rely on that help us cope with our fears. The ability to be courageous despite our fear. The ability to regret. The ability to feel. The ability to be kind. These traits work together, along with fear, to make us better people.

Next year is going to be a great year for you, Julian. I can feel it. I have faith in you! Just give everyone a chance and you'll do fine. Best of luck to you!

Sometimes, all a kid needs is a little push to have a revelation. I'm not saying I was that push. I think Julian's very wise grandmother was. The point is: everyone's got a story. The challenge with some kids is to be patient enough to listen.

—Mr. Browne

AUGUST

That is the
beginning of
knowledge—
the discovery of
something we do
not understand.

—Frank Herbert

Far away in the sunshine are
my highest aspirations.
I may not reach them, but
I can look up and see their
beauty, believe in them, and
try to follow where they lead.

—Louisa May Alcott

Just as there is no loss of basic
energy in the universe, so no
thought or action is without
its effects, present or ultimate,
seen or unseen, felt or unfelt.

—Norman Cousins

I am part of all that I have met.

—Alfred, Lord Tennyson

Do not seek to follow in the footsteps of the wise. Seek what they sought.

—Matsuo Bashō

Courage doesn't
always roar.
Sometimes
courage is the
quiet voice at the
end of the
day saying,
"I will try
again tomorrow."

—Mary Anne Radmacher

The more
I wonder,
the more
I love.

—Alice Walker

You can never
cross the ocean
unless you have
the courage
to lose sight of
the shore.

—André Gide

One of the most essential
prerequisites to happiness is
unbounded tolerance.

—A. C. Fifield

You don't get harmony when everyone sings the same note.

—Doug Floyd

ALWAYS BE ON
THE LOOKOUT FOR
THE PRESENCE
OF WONDER.

—E. B. White

Life is not meant to be easy, my child; but take courage: it can be delightful.

—George Bernard Shaw

I cannot do all the good that the world needs, but the world needs all the good that I can do.

—Jana Stanfield

—Unknown

The splendid achievements
of the intellect, like the soul,
are everlasting.

—Sallust

The sage has
one advantage:
He is immortal.
If this is not his
century, many
others will be.

—Baltasar Gracián

THE THINGS THAT MAKE ME
DIFFERENT ARE THE THINGS
THAT MAKE ME **ME.**

—Piglet (A. A. Milne)

We measure minds by their stature; it would be better to estimate them by their beauty.

—Joseph Joubert

It always seems
impossible until
it is done.

—Nelson Mandela

A wise man can
learn more from
a foolish
question than a
fool can learn from
a wise answer.

—Bruce Lee

If you want to go quickly,
go alone. If you want to go far,
go together.

—African proverb

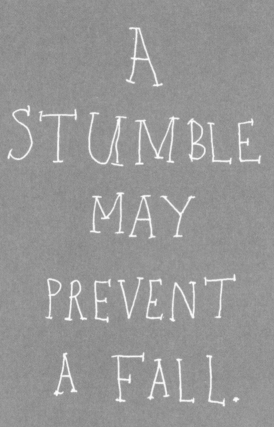

A STUMBLE MAY PREVENT A FALL.

—English proverb

Whatever is worth doing at all
is worth doing well.

——Philip Dormer Stanhope

Yesternight the
sun went hence,
And yet is here
today.

—John Donne

Kindness, like a boomerang,
always returns.

—Unknown

Just keep swimming no matter how hard the current.

—Ava

Wisdom is like a
baobab tree:
No one person can
embrace it, but
a tribe can.

—African proverb

The butterfly counts not
months but moments, and
has time enough.

—Rabindranath Tagore

A good name will shine forever.

—African proverb

Very little is needed to make a happy life.

——Marcus Aurelius

Nothing in Nature is
unbeautiful.

—Alfred, Lord Tennyson

K indness can spread from person to person like glitter. Anyone who's ever introduced glitter into any kind of art project at school knows exactly of what I speak. You can't shake it off you. You pass it on to the next person. Its sparkling remnants linger for days. And for each tiny dot you find, you know that a hundred more have seemingly vanished. But where did they go? What happens to all that glitter?

I had a boy in my class last year whose name was August. He was quite special, and not because of his face. There was just something about his indomitable spirit that captured me (and a lot of the people around him). The year turned out to be a raging success for Auggie. I was very glad about that. Now, I'm not naive enough to think that a happy ending to a fifth-grade year will guarantee him a happy life. I know he'll have more than his share of challenges. But what I gleaned from his triumphant year was this: he has what he needs inside of him to stand up to life's challenges. Auggie will have a beautiful life. That's my prediction.

I got an email from him the other day that kind of validates this prediction.

To: tbrowne@beecherschool.edu
Fr: apullman@beecherschool.edu
Re: The postcard

Hey there, Mr. Browne! Long time no speak!

I hope you're having a great summer! I sent you my precept last month. Hope you got it. It had a giant fish on it. From Montauk.

So I'm writing to thank you for sending me Julian's note in the mail. Whoa, I did not see that coming! When I opened your letter I was, like, what is this other envelope? And then I opened it and I saw the handwriting. And I was like, no way, is Julian sending me mean notes again? You probably don't know this, but Julian left some really mean notes in my locker last year. Anyway, it turned out that this note wasn't a mean note! It was actually an apology! Can you believe it? It was sealed, so maybe you didn't read it, but this is what the note said:

DEAR AUGGIE,

I WANT TO APOLOGIZE FOR THE STUFF I DID LAST YEAR. I'VE BEEN THINKING ABOUT IT A LOT. YOU DIDN'T DESERVE IT. I WISH I COULD HAVE A DO-OVER. I WOULD BE NICER. I HOPE YOU DON'T REMEMBER HOW MEAN I WAS WHEN YOU'RE EIGHTY YEARS OLD. HAVE A NICE LIFE.

—JULIAN

PS: IF YOU'RE THE ONE WHO TOLD MR. TUSHMAN ABOUT THE NOTES, DON'T WORRY, I'M NOT MAD.

I'm kind of in a state of shock about this note. By the way, he's wrong about me being the one who told Mr. Tushman. It wasn't me (or Summer or Jack). Maybe Mr. Tushman really does have microscopic spy satellites tracking everything we do in school! Maybe he's even watching me . . . right NOW! If you're listening, Mr. Tushman, I hope you had a great summer! Anyway, just goes to show, you never know with people!

To: apullman@beecherschool.edu
Fr: tbrowne@beecherschool.edu
Re: Re: The postcard

Hey there, Auggie (and Mr. Tushman, if you're listening). I just wanted to write you a quick little note to say how happy I am that you got some closure with Julian. There's nothing that can make up for what he put you through, but there must be some satisfaction in knowing that he's grown as a person because of you. You're right: you just never know with people. See you next month!

To: tbrowne@beecherschool.edu
Fr: apullman@beecherschool.edu
Re: The truth revealed?

Yeah, it's true. You never know! I showed my mom the postcard and she just about fainted. "Will wonders never cease!" she said. Then I told Jack and he was like, "Did you check the postcard for poison?" You know Jack. But seriously, I don't know what might have motivated Julian to write the apology, but I really appreciated it. The one thing I still don't know is: WHO TOLD MR. TUSHMAN ABOUT THE NOTES? Was it you, Mr. Browne?

To: apullman@beecherschool.edu
Fr: tbrowne@beecherschool.edu
Re: Re: The truth revealed?

Ha! I promise, it wasn't me who told Mr. Tushman. I had no idea about those awful notes! It may just be one of those mysteries that never get solved!

To: tbrowne@beecherschool.edu
Fr: apullman@beecherschool.edu
Re: Re: The truth revealed?

So here's the thing about glitter: once it's out of the bottle, there's just no way of putting it back. It's the same with kindness. Once it pours out of your soul, there's no way of containing it. It just continues to spread from person to person, a shining, sparkling, wonderful thing.

—Mr. Browne

SEPTEMBER

When given the
choice between
being right or
being kind,
choose kind.

—Dr. Wayne W. Dyer

Begin, be bold, and venture to be wise.

—Horace

The wisest men
follow their own
course.

—Euripides

Life isn't about
finding yourself.
Life is about
creating yourself.

—George Bernard Shaw

Beauty is not in the
face; beauty is a
light in the heart.

—Kahlil Gibran

The secret of getting things done is to act!

—Dante Alighieri

Accept what you
can't change.
Change what you
can't accept.

——Unknown

You can't have
a rainbow
without
a little bit
of Rain

—Unknown

An act of kindness never dies,
but extends the invisible
undulations of its influence
over the breadth of centuries.

—Father Faber

If there is no struggle, there is no progress.

—Frederick Douglass

Every hour of
the light and DARK
is a miracle.

—Walt Whitman

Never hesitate to tell the
truth. And never, ever give
in or give up.

—Bella Abzug

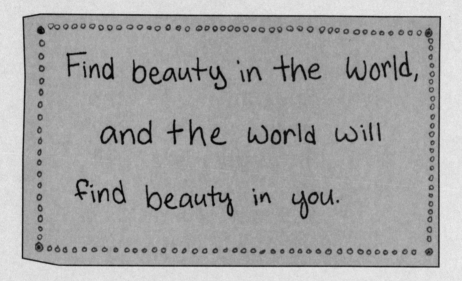

Find beauty in the world, and the world will find beauty in you.

—Zöe

Sometimes rejection in
life is really redirection.

—Tavis Smiley

I don't believe you have to be
better than everybody else.
I believe you have to be better
than you thought you could be.

—Ken Venturi

Being nice is being cool!

—Alexis

What is a friend?
A single soul dwelling
in two bodies.

—Aristotle

Sometimes
the questions
are complicated
but the
answers
are simple.

—Dr. Seuss

You are a conductor

of light.

—Sir Arthur Conan Doyle

Knowledge is love
and light and vision.

—Helen Keller

Strong people don't put others down. They lift them up.

—Michael P. Watson

To him whose elastic and vigorous
thought keeps pace with the sun, the
day is a perpetual morning.

—Henry David Thoreau

I believe that unarmed truth
and unconditional love will
have the final word.

—Martin Luther King, Jr.

Treat others
how you
want to be
treated.

—Proverb

Nothing happens unless first a dream.

—Carl Sandburg

Doing your best is the best you can do.

—Riley

Come forth into the light
of things. Let Nature be
your teacher.

—William Wordsworth

Ah! the immensity of the
value of persons to each
other, and of kind deeds
and affectionate inventions
between them, for the
making of happiness!

—James Vila Blake, *More Than Kin*

You are
your own
little light,
shine bright
so everyone
can see.

—Elizabeth

There are always flowers
for those who want to
see them.

—Henri Matisse

I've always thought that good teaching is about illumination. Sure, we teach things kids might not know, but a lot of the time, we're just shedding light on the stuff they already do know. There's a lot of that happening in the fifth grade. Kids know how to read, but I'm trying to get them to *love* reading. Kids know how to write, but I'm trying to inspire them to express themselves better. In both instances, they have the materials they need already inside them: I'm just here to guide them a bit, to shed a little light. To illume.

That's one of the reasons I like to start every year off with the Dr. Wayne W. Dyer precept about "choosing kind." The kids are all new to middle school. A lot of them don't know each other. I think of this precept as a preemptive strike against much of what is to come, an inception in their psyches. I plant a little notion of kindness so that at least it's there, this seedling buried inside them. Will it take root? Will it flower? Who knows? But either way, I've done my deed.

> *When given the choice between being right or being kind, choose kind.*
>
> —Dr. Wayne W. Dyer

This particular quote usually provokes days of discussion after I introduce it. I often start my conversation about precepts with a general survey: Do you like the precept? Does it apply to how you live your life? What do you think it means?

Then I start talking about the obvious benefits of the precept. If everyone adopted that quote as his or her own personal precept, I ask them, wouldn't the world be a better place? Imagine if nations adopted it as a mandate—wouldn't there be fewer conflicts? Some kids agree, adding that if nations chose to be kind instead of right, it might even end world hunger. Other kids argue that being wealthy doesn't have anything to do with being right.

I sometimes ask the students how hard it would be for them to choose to back down from an argument with their moms or dads or siblings if they knew they were right and the other person was wrong. Would they give in just to let the other person save face? Why? Why not? This part of the discussion is often *very* lively!

It's not so simple a thing to choose to be kind. It's one thing to back down from an argument with someone you love—a friend, say—because you don't see the point in "winning" the argument at the cost of your friend's feelings. But what if you believe in something that no one else believes in? What if you're the only one who knows you're right? Should you back down, just to be kind? What if you were Galileo and you knew you were right about the planets revolving around the sun, even though the rest of the world thought you were crazy—would you back down? What if you were living in the 1950s and you were against segregation—would you back down, just to be polite? What if you were standing up for something you believed in—would you really want to back down, just for the sake of kindness? No! You'd stand up and fight, right?

All this will often lead to some kids questioning whether the precept is really good, after all. At this point, I always suggest to them that maybe the most important words in the precept aren't "kind" or "right." Maybe the most important word in that whole sentence is the word "choose." You have the choice. What do you choose?

As I said, my job is to plant the notion in your minds, kids. Inception. Once the seed is planted, all I try to do is keep shedding some light on it. And watch it grow. In time, you'll begin shining your own lights, and then—watch out, world!

—Mr. Browne

OCTOBER

Your deeds are your monuments.

—Inscription on an Egyptian tomb

I do not believe in a fate that falls on men however they act; but I do believe in a fate that falls on them unless they act.

—G. K. Chesterton

It is better to be in
the dark with a friend
than to be in the light
without one.

—John

What you do
every day
matters more
than what you
do every once
in a while.

—Unknown

Don't cry
because it's
OVER,
smile
because
IT happened.

—Dr. Seuss

Be bold enough to use your
voice, brave enough to listen
to your heart, and strong
enough to live the life
you've always imagined.

—Unknown

Great opportunities
to help others seldom
come, but small ones
surround us every day.

—Sally Koch

INVITE OTHERS TO
WONDER WITH YOU.

—Austin Kleon, *Steal Like an Artist*

Kindness is the golden chain by which society is bound together.

—Johann Wolfgang von Goethe

If you can't change your
fate, change your attitude.

—Amy Tan

Rise above the little things.

—John Burroughs

Inward happiness
almost always
follows a kind
action.

—Father Faber

I ask not for a lighter burden, but for broader shoulders.

—Jewish proverb

Be yourself, you will not get a second chance to.

—Daniel

Love truth, but
pardon error.

—Voltaire

What makes night
within us may leave
stars.

—Victor Hugo

Normal is a setting

on a washing machine.

—Unknown

The best angle from which to approach any problem is the try-angle.

—Unknown

Don't choose the one who is beautiful to the world. But rather, choose the one who makes your world beautiful.

—Harry Styles

Seek not,
my soul,
immortal life,
but make the
most of what is
within thy reach.

—Pindar

We make our world
significant by the courage of
our questions and the depth
of our answers.

—Carl Sagan

Fashion your life as a garden of beautiful deeds.

—Unknown

Be kind, for everyone you meet is fighting a hard battle.

—Ian Maclaren

The soul aids the body, and at certain moments, raises it. It is the only bird which bears up its own cage.

—Victor Hugo

Everything has its wonders,
even darkness and silence,
and I learn, whatever state I
am in, therein to be content.

—Helen Keller

It is only with the heart that one can see rightly; what is essential is invisible to the eye.

—Antoine de Saint Exupéry

Even the darkest hour has only sixty minutes.

—Morris Mandel

The mind is everything. What you think you become.

—Unknown

Constant kindness can
accomplish much.
As the sun makes ice
melt, kindness causes
misunderstanding, mistrust,
and hostility to evaporate.

——Albert Schweitzer

Find out what
your gift is,
and nurture it.

—Katy Perry

The way to have a
friend is to be a friend.

—Hugh Black

I read an article a few years ago about a couple of biologists who studied a troop of baboons over a twenty-year period. This particular troop was full of very aggressive "alpha" male baboons that routinely attacked and bullied the females and weaker males in the troop, depriving them of access to food sources. This proved unexpectedly advantageous one day when the alpha males ate infected meat. They all died, but the females and weaker males survived. Within a short time, the baboon troop took on a totally new dynamic. They were significantly less aggressive, more social, and, behaviorally, less "stressed" than before. What's more, these changes lasted long after that first generation of "nicer" baboons died out. New baboons joining the troop assimilated the less aggressive behavior and passed it on. The transmission of "kindness"—if such it could be called—took root. And it grew.

So, why am I talking about baboons? No, I'm not about to compare a class of fifth graders to baboons, don't worry! But I *am* going to go out on a limb (ha, no pun intended) and draw the following lesson: a small, dominant clique can set the tone for a group. Ask any teacher. If you're lucky enough to have a few alpha kids in your class who can set a positive tone for the year, you're in for a good year. Conversely, if you happen to get a few dominant kids who are bent on making trouble, then fasten your seat belts!

Last year turned out to be a great year. Although the usual fifth-grade antics were intensified by the

Auggie and Julian "rift," which ended well for Auggie, there was little drama among the girls. Summer, with her self-confident, sprightly nature, was a great influence. I had another student, Charlotte, who was also very sweet. We had this exchange via Google Docs the other day:

Hi, Mr. Browne. I'm writing an article for the school newspaper and was wondering if I could interview you about precepts. Hope you have the time.

Hi, Charlotte. I'd be happy to help.

Oh yay! Thank you! First of all, did you get my precept over the summer? "It's not enough to be friendly. You have to be a friend."

Yes, I did! Thank you for sending it. I liked it very much.

Thanks! You're probably wondering why I chose that precept.

Yes, actually. I'm very curious.

Oh, well, here's why. Do you remember at graduation, how Auggie won the Beecher Award? I thought that was so cool because he really deserved it. But I also kind of thought that other people should have won it, too. Like Jack. And Summer. They were such good friends to Auggie—even in the beginning, when kids were running away from him.

Hey, this part isn't going to be in the newspaper, right?

Totally not!

Just checking! Sorry to interrupt.

No prob. It's just that I started thinking about how I had never really gotten to know Auggie myself. Like, I was nice to him. I said hello in the hallways. I was never mean to him. But, you know, I never did what Summer did. I never sat down with him at lunchtime. I never defended him to my friends, like Jack did.

Don't be too hard on yourself, Charlotte. You were always very nice.

Yeah, but "being nice" is not the same as "choosing kind."

I see your point.

This year, I started sitting at the "summer" table. It's me, Auggie, Summer, Jack, Maya, and Reid. I know some kids still don't like being around Auggie, but that's their problem, right?

Very right.

So anyway, back to the newspaper article. I was wondering if you could share with readers why you first started collecting precepts? What inspired you?

Hmm. I guess I first came upon the notion of collecting precepts when I was in college. I happened upon the writings of Sir Thomas Browne, a seventeenth-century man of all trades, and found his work deeply moving.

Seriously? His name was Thomas Browne?

Incredible coincidence, isn't it?

So when did you start teaching precepts to kids?

Not too long afterward, when I started student teaching. Actually, it's funny that you're asking me these questions, because I've been thinking about putting together a book of all the precepts I've collected over the years, along with some essays in which I touch upon some of the very questions you're asking me.

Really? That is such an awesome idea! I would totally buy that book!

Good! I'm glad you like it.

So I think those were the only questions I had. I'm looking forward to reading your book when it comes out.

Thank you. Bye, Charlotte!

What I loved most about this exchange was the idea that Charlotte herself realized the profound impact of kindness.

I began this essay with a true story of baboons, and ended with the story of a girl. In both, the transmission of kindness had taken root. What can biologists and teachers alike do but marvel at its impact?

—Mr. Browne

NOVEMBER

Have no friends not
equal to yourself.

—Confucius

It is a rough
road that leads
to the heights
of greatness.

—Seneca

No one is good
at everything
but everyone
is good at
Something.

—Clark

Turn your wounds
into wisdom.

—Oprah Winfrey

In kindness is encompassed
every variety of wisdom.

—Ernesto Sábato

Don't strive for love, be it.

—Hugh Prather

Good friends are like stars.
You don't always see them,
but you know they're
always there.

—Unknown

When life
gives you
lemons,
make orange
juice.
Be unique!

—J.J.

If opportunity doesn't knock, build a door.

—Milton Berle

O world, I am in tune
with every note of
thy great harmony.

—Marcus Aurelius

My religion is
very simple.
My religion is
kindness.

—Dalai Lama

Today, fill
your cup of
life with
sunshine and
laughter.

—Dodinsky

Life is like sailing. You can
use any wind to go
in any direction.

—Robert Brault

If you're lucky
enough to be different,
don't ever change.

—Taylor Swift

It costs nothing

to be nice.

—Harry Styles

To succeed in life, you need
three things: a wishbone,
a backbone and a funny bone.

—Reba McEntire

The devotion of thought to an honest achievement makes the achievement possible.

—Mary Baker Eddy

When you are living the
best version of yourself, you
inspire others to live the
best versions of themselves.

—Steve Maraboli

The happiness of life is made up of minute fractions—the little, soon forgotten charities of a kiss or smile, a kind look, a heartfelt compliment, and the countless infinitesimals of pleasurable and genial feeling.

—Samuel Taylor Coleridge

If you don't Know, you should ask.

—Hailey

—*Les Misérables, The Musical* (Alain Boublil)

Kindness can become its own motive. We are made kind by being kind.

—Eric Hoffer

What this
world needs
is a new
kind of
army—the
army of the
kind.

—Cleveland Amory

Let us be grateful to people
who make us happy. They are
the charming gardeners who
make our souls blossom.

—Marcel Proust

And the song, from
beginning to end,
I found again in the
heart of a friend.

—Henry Wadsworth Longfellow

Happiness is a perfume
you cannot pour on
others without getting a
few drops on yourself.

—Unknown

Good deeds can lead to more good deeds which can lead to more good deeds that will eventually lead back to you!

—Nicolas

There are no shortcuts to
any place worth going.

—Beverly Sills

WHEN
IT'S DARK,
BE THE
ONE WHO

TURNS

ON

THE

LIGHT.

—Joseph

Big shots are only
little shots who
keep shooting.

—Christopher Morley

One of my students dressed up as Frodo for Halloween last month, which caused me to casually make this offhand remark: "I love Frodo, but, let's face it, Samwise Gamgee is the greatest hero of Middle-earth."

Well, you would have thought I'd just said we were doing away with Halloween or something, judging from the number of gasps and "No way!"s I got. I don't remember the last time one of my statements generated so much controversy in my classroom! Although the class was more or less evenly split between Aragorn and Frodo as the greatest hero—with some Gandalf advocates—not one person agreed with me about Samwise.

So I tried to elaborate on my crazy thinking. Sam, I reminded them, was the loyal companion to Frodo through thick and thin. All those times Frodo was about to give up, Sam kept him going. When Frodo couldn't carry the ring anymore, Sam took Frodo on his back across the desolate plains of Mordor. When Sam thought Frodo was dead, he took the ring himself and set about to destroy it. And when the ring started working its seduction on him, Sam was one of the few creatures in all of Middle-earth who were able to resist the temptation. In a way, I told the kids, Sam stands as a shining example of the four virtues. In classical antiquity, it was believed that to be a truly great person, one should have in equal proportions the following four virtues:

WISDOM: prudence, as garnered from experience, or the ability to respond appropriately to any given situation.

JUSTICE: the ability to fight for what is right. The perpetual and constant will to render to each one his right.

COURAGE: the ability to confront fear, uncertainty, or intimidation.

TEMPERANCE: the ability to practice moderation— even when tempted to give in to one's own self-interest or desire. Temperance is the art of self-control.

Samwise Gamgee is the epitome of all those virtues, I told my students. But then they pointed out that he wasn't especially wise, which I had to give them. And he didn't really live for Justice, which I had to give them, too. Ultimately, we decided, as a whole, that Sam stood for Temperance. He never gave in to his own wishful thinking, but stood fast and firm to help his friends.

"So what other fictional heroes can we think of that stand for the other virtues?" I asked the kids. And this is where the fun began! I gave them a couple of days to do some research, and then we had our class discussion.

For Wisdom, the most common name offered was: Yoda. "Come on!" I rebuked in a comical way. "Really? That's such an obvious answer." I told them I thought the wisest character, if we were going the Star Wars route, was Luke Skywalker. Not at first, of course. But after Luke learned to master his own feelings and gained a deeper insight into others' feelings, he became a calm, cool, and collected Jedi Knight, who was smart enough to take on the dark side of the Force. They were not convinced. Apparently, Luke holds less appeal for the under-forty crowd than Yoda.

For Justice, we turned to The Chronicles of Narnia. Edmund, who actually becomes King Edmund the Just after redeeming himself, was the fairly unanimous choice.

For Courage, we went to the world of superheroes. A big debate arose about Superman versus Batman. Superman, it was pointed out, was very courageous, but then again, he was impervious to everything, except Kryptonite (and how many people carry Kryptonite in their pocket, right?). Batman, on the other hand, was just an ordinary guy with lots of gadgets, who was seriously brave. This remained an unresolved dispute, and just may be for the rest of time.

I actually used that great rivalry to bring up one of my all-time favorites: Achilles versus Hector. It was a fun way for me to introduce this ancient feud to those who hadn't heard about it. Basically, I told them, Achilles was the greatest hero of the Greeks. His mother was a goddess, and when he was a baby, she dunked him in the river Styx and made him invincible—except for his heel, which was where she was holding him. What's more, Achilles's armor was forged by a god, making him even more impossible to defeat. And to top it all off, Achilles was the best-trained warrior of all time: the dude liked to fight! Hector, on the other hand, who was the champion of the Trojans, did not like to fight. Nor did he have a goddess for a mother or a god to forge his armor. In fact, he was just an ordinary guy who was especially good with a sword, fighting to save his home when one thousand Greek ships invaded his shores.

Then I told the kids about the epic fight between Achilles and Hector. They were so excited by it! Who says kids can't be taught the classics anymore?

The final virtue to be debated was Temperance. What character from a book or movie best embodied the art of self-control? We turned to the world of Harry Potter for that one. Seems like Harry himself, though sometimes something of a rule-breaker, never abused his unique powers for self-gain. As one student said, he could have used his invisibility cloak a hundred times to do bad things, but he didn't. Instead, he used his powers for the greater good. That's the great lesson Rowling teaches.

It was quite a wonderful teaching day for me, one that sprang completely from a boy in a costume. Although I may have veered off-topic for a day, I think the lessons learned were more valuable than anything in today's curriculum.

Teachers need the freedom to teach—freedom they can't have if they're only teaching so their students can pass tests. I'm pretty sure my students won't find anything about Hector on the Common Core tests. I'm equally sure that what they learned about Wisdom, Justice, Courage, and Temperance may stay with them for the rest of their lives.

—Mr. Browne

DECEMBER

Fortune favors the bold.

—Virgil

Kindness is
difficult to give
away because
it keeps
coming back.

—Marcel Proust

The smallest
good deed is better
than the grandest
intention.

—Unknown

I'm not afraid of storms, for I'm learning how to sail my ship.

—Louisa May Alcott

On that best portion of

a good man's life,

His little, nameless,

unremembered, acts

Of kindness and of love.

—William Wordsworth

By perseverance,
the snail reached
the ark.

—Charles Spurgeon

I believe that every human mind feels pleasure in doing good to another.

—Thomas Jefferson

I've learned
that life is like
a book. Sometimes
we must close a
chapter and begin
the next one.

—Hanz

You're like a bird,

Spread your wings

and Soar above

the Clouds.

—Mairead

The sun does not
shine for a few trees
and flowers, but for
the wide world's joy

—Henry Ward Beecher

All our dreams can
come true—if we
have the courage to
pursue them.

—Walt Disney

Injustice anywhere is a threat
to justice everywhere.

—Martin Luther King, Jr.

You are never too old
to set another goal
or to dream a new
dream.

—C. S. Lewis

Life is like an
ice-cream cone; you
have to lick
it one day at a time.

—Charles M. Schulz

Accept what you have
and treat it well.

—Brody

For beautiful eyes, look

for the good in others;

for beautiful lips, speak

only words of kindness;

and for poise, walk

with the knowledge

that you are never alone.

—Audrey Hepburn

True wisdom lies in gathering the precious things out of each day as it goes by.

—E. S. Bouton

Nothing will work
unless you do.

—Maya Angelou

EVEN THE
SMALLEST
PERSON
CAN CHANGE
THE COURSE
OF THE FUTURE.

—J.R.R. Tolkien

To give service to a
single heart by a single act
is better than a thousand
heads bowing in prayer.

—Mahatma Gandhi

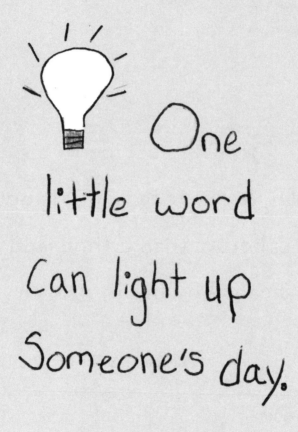

One little word can light up someone's day.

—Ainsley

Do your little bit of
good where you are;
it's those little bits of
good put together that
overwhelm the world.

—Desmond Tutu

Happiness resides
not in possessions,
and not in gold.
Happiness dwells
in the soul.

—Democritus

Goodness does not consist

in greatness, but greatness

in goodness.

—Athenaeus

A single sunbeam is enough to drive away many shadows.

—St. Francis of Assisi

Amid life's quests, there seems but worthy one: to do men good.

—Gamaliel Bailey

A big heart
is determined
to make other
hearts grow.

—Christina

Happiness is someone to love, something to do, and something to hope for.

—Chinese proverb

We didn't all come over on the same ship, but we're all in the same boat.

—Bernard Baruch

Dream your dreams,
but when you act,
plant your feet firmly on
the ground.

—Noel Clarasó

Let us always meet each other

with a smile. . . .

—Mother Teresa

MYSTERIES

December. The end of the year. The start of a new year. A chance to remember. A chance to look forward. It was nice hearing from some of my former students: Auggie. Summer. Charlotte. And, of course, the biggest surprise to me of all—Julian. That is, until I got this short and pithy email from Amos, one of my students from last year. This boy, who was generally a quiet kid, not one to speak up in class, surprised us all when he came to the rescue of Auggie and Jack at the nature retreat last year. He led the charge and showed great leadership. Sometimes kids don't even know they're leaders until they start to lead.

When I got this email, it was the answer to one little mystery (that I know I wasn't the only person to wonder about).

To: tbrowne@beecherschool.edu
Fr: amosconti@wazoomail.com
Subject: My precept—at last!

Hey, Mr. B, hope you have a happy holiday! Sorry I didn't get around to sending you a postcard over the summer. Had a lot going on, you know? But here goes: "Don't try too hard to be cool. It always shows, and that's uncool."

What do you think? Cool, huh? I won't explain what my precept means because it's pretty obvious, right? I mean, you probably know who I'm talking about, right? Hee-hee-hee.

No, seriously. Last year was tough, man! Lots of drama! Yo, I'm not into drama, usually. That's why I was so sick and tired of that stuff going on with Julian. There's not a lot of drama this year, which is good. No one bothers Auggie anymore. I mean, a little, but not too much. Let's face it, people are always going to stare a bit. But Auggie's a tough little dude and no one messes with him anymore.

Okay, look, I'm going to let you in on a little secret. Ready? So, you know how Julian got in big trouble for leaving mean notes in Auggie's locker, right? Everyone says it's the real reason Julian's not coming back to school next year. I've even heard a few people say he was actually suspended for it! Anyway, the big mystery is: how did Mr. Tushman even find out about the notes? Auggie didn't tell him. Jack didn't tell him. Summer didn't tell him. Julian didn't tell him. Miles didn't tell him. And Henry didn't tell him. You know how I know? Because . . . drumroll here . . . it was me! I'm the one who told Mr. Tushman about the notes. Didn't see that coming, did you?

So let me explain a bit. What happened was that Henry and Miles knew Julian was leaving the mean notes. They told me about the notes but made me swear not to tell anyone. But after they told me, I thought it just really sucked big-time that Julian was being so mean to Auggie. It was kind of like bullying. And even though I swore to Henry and Miles that I wouldn't say anything, I needed to tell Tushman about it so he could do something to protect Auggie. Hey, I'm an upstander—not a bystander! Little dudes like Auggie need guys like me to step it up, right?

So that's the story, Mr. B. Don't go telling anyone, though! I don't want to be accused of being, you know, a "snitch." Then again, I guess I don't really care. I know I did the right thing.

Keep warm, Mr. B! It's cold out there!

Yeah, maybe it's cold out there, but this warmed my heart completely. I have to admit: I did not see that one coming. Just goes to show, everyone really does have a story to tell. And most people, at least in my experience, are a little more noble than they think they are.

—Mr. Browne

JANUARY 1: **SIR THOMAS BROWNE** (10/19/1605–10/19/1682) was an English physician, philosopher, and author who wrote about the natural world, science, and religion. He is well known for *Religio Medici*, his reflections on being a man of faith as well as science, and *Pseudodoxia Epidemica*, an exploration—and debunking—of the accepted tenets of his day. In a century known for its religious wars and persecution, Browne was a polymath whose kindness and tolerance extended toward people of all races and creeds. The quote in this book is from *Religio Medici*, 1642.

JANUARY 2: **ROALD DAHL** (9/13/1916–11/23/1990) was a British writer best remembered for his children's books, which are known for their black humor and wit. His most famous works are *Charlie and the Chocolate Factory*, *James and the Giant Peach*, *Matilda*, *The BFG*, and *Fantastic Mr. Fox*, but he also co-wrote the script for *Chitty Chitty Bang Bang* and other films. The quote in this book is from *The Minpins*, 1991.

JANUARY 3: **HENRY JAMES** (4/15/1843–2/28/1916) was born in New York City but spent most of his life in England. He was a prolific writer whose novels, including *The Portrait of a Lady*, *The Golden Bowl*, and *Washington Square*—which was set in the neighborhood where he was born—are closely identified with the literary realism movement.

JANUARY 4: **JOHN DONNE** (1/22/1572–3/31/1631) was one of the greatest English poets of all time. Later termed a metaphysical poet, Donne wrote about subjects as diverse as religion—he was born a Catholic at a time when Catholics were out of favor in England—and romantic love. He had twelve children with his wife, Anne More, who died in childbirth at the age of thirty-three. The quotes in this book are from *Devotions Upon Emergent Occasions*, 1624 (January 4) and from "Sweetest Love, I Do Not Go" (August 24).

JANUARY 5: **ELZIE CRISLER SEGAR** (12/8/1894–10/13/1938) was an American cartoonist whose best-known character was Popeye, whom he introduced in a *Thimble Theatre* comic strip on January 17, 1929. Popeye is a pipe-smoking, spinach-eating sailor man who loves his girlfriend, Olive Oyl, and his adopted son, Swee'Pea. It is still in publication today, making it one of the longest-running strips in syndication of all time. The quote in this book is from *Popeye*, 1933.

JOHN LENNON (10/9/1940–12/8/1980) and **PAUL McCARTNEY** (6/18/1942–present) were two of the four musicians who comprised the world-famous British pop-rock group the Beatles. Lennon and McCartney, who started writing songs together as teenagers, wrote most of the songs performed by the Beatles (approximately 180 songs), including "Help!," "A Hard Day's Night," "All You Need Is Love," "Eleanor Rigby," "Lucy in the Sky with Diamonds," and "Let It Be." The quote in this book is from "All You Need Is Love," 1967.

MARK TWAIN (11/30/1835–4/21/1910) was born Samuel Langhorne Clemens in Missouri, the setting for his iconic books *The Adventures of Tom Sawyer* and *Adventures of Huckleberry Finn*. He was a prolific writer but also held other jobs at various points in his lifetime: typesetter, steamboat pilot (his pen name was borrowed from a pilot's term for safe passage), miner, and journalist. He supported the abolition of slavery and had a deep interest in science and technology, counting Nikola Tesla, the renowned physicist, as one of his closest friends.

CARL SAGAN (11/9/1934–12/20/1996) was an American astronomer whose work led to several discoveries about the atmosphere of planets in our solar system. He was a consultant for NASA for decades, but is most well remembered for his scientific contributions to the search for extraterrestrial life, in which he was a strong believer. He wrote many bestselling books, including *Cosmos*, and hosted a television series that helped popularize scientific subjects, such as the big bang theory and the origin of life. The quotes in this book are from a *Newsweek* interview, 1977 (January 8), from episode 5 of *Cosmos*, 1995 (July 29), and from his book *Cosmos*, 1980 (October 21).

KAHLIL GIBRAN (1/6/1883–4/10/1931) was a writer and artist best known for *The Prophet*, published in 1923, which is composed of twenty-six essays dealing with aspects of the human condition, such as love, death, joy and sorrow, friendship, and the nature of good and evil. It has been translated into over forty languages and has never gone out of print. Gibran is considered to be the third-bestselling poet of all time, behind William Shakespeare and Lao Tzu.

PAUL BRANDT (7/21/1972–present) is a Canadian country singer/songwriter. This quote is from "There's a World Out There," written by Donald Ewing II and Kent Blazy.

ANNE FRANK (6/12/1929–February 1945) was born Anneliese Marie Frank in Frankfurt, Germany, to Otto and Edith Frank.

Following the victory of the Nazi Party in the 1933 elections, Otto moved the family to Amsterdam to escape the growing anti-Semitism. However, the Germans occupied Holland in 1940. In 1942, the Franks were forced into hiding, living in concealed rooms in the building in which Otto Frank had worked. Those two years in hiding—until the day the family was arrested and sent to concentration camps—were documented carefully by thirteen-year-old Anne in her diary. Anne and her sister, Margot, died within days of each other in Bergen-Belsen, only months before the British liberation of the camp. Anne's diary was published several years after her death. Anne's message of hopefulness in the inherent goodness of man, despite all the tragedies that befell her, remains one of the most beloved works of literature of the twentieth century. The quote in this book is from *The Diary of Anne Frank*, 1947.

JANUARY 14: **LAO TZU** (sixth century BC) was a Chinese philosopher whose work the *Tao Te Ching* is the sacred text at the heart of the spiritual practice of Taoism. The Tao, which translates to "the way," gives directives about how to live a good and happy life through the practice of meditation, stillness, and harmony with nature.

JANUARY 15: **PAUL VALÉRY** (10/30/1871–7/20/1945) was a French poet and philosopher. While his early acclaim came from his poetical works, such as *Charmes*, it was his notebooks, *Cahiers*, for which he is best known today. These were his reflections on subjects such as math and science, and his musings on human nature.

JANUARY 17: **J.R.R. (JOHN RONALD REUEL) TOLKIEN** (1/3/1892– 9/2/1973) was an English writer and professor who is best remembered for his works about the fantasy realm of Middle-earth, composed of *The Hobbit*, The Lord of the Rings trilogy, and *The Silmarrillion*. An accomplished linguist, Tolkien was largely inspired by Old English, Germanic, and Norse literature and mythology, such as *Beowulf*, the *Elder Edda*, and the *Nibelungenlied*. The quotes in this book are from *The Lord of the Rings*, 1954.

JANUARY 18: **ANNIE LENNOX** (12/25/1954–present) is a Scottish singer, songwriter, and political activist. In the 1980s, she was part of the successful musical duo Eurythmics. She was honored as an Officer of the Order of the British Empire by Queen Elizabeth II in 2011 for her many years of charity work, particularly in raising awareness of HIV/AIDS and its effect on African women and children.

A. A. (ALAN ALEXANDER) MILNE (1/18/1882–1/31/1956) was an essayist, novelist, and playwright before penning his hugely successful children's books based on the adventures of a teddy bear called Winnie-the-Pooh. Named after the author's son, Christopher Robin is the young boy who lives in the Hundred Acre Wood with Winnie-the-Pooh, Piglet, Tigger, and their friends, almost all of which were based on his son's stuffed animals. The quotes in this book are from *Winnie-the-Pooh*, 1926.

HENRY BURTON (1840–1930) was born in England, but moved to America as a boy. He became a Methodist minister after graduating from Beloit College, but entered the Wesleyan ministry upon his return to England in 1865. Remembered for his hymns, Burton said the inspiration of his most famous one, "Pass It On," came from a true story told to him by his father-in-law about how, as a young man, he'd been short of money on board a steamer returning home to England. The ship's steward gave the young man the money he needed, saying that many years before, the young man's father had rescued him from a similar plight. The quote in this book is from "Have You Had a Kindness Shown."

THE ROCKY HORROR PICTURE SHOW: This 1975 tribute to science fiction and B movies became a cult classic when audiences began participating at midnight showings in New York City in 1976 by repeating lines and shouting responses at the screen—as well as dressing up as the characters and performing as the movie played. It remains one of the best-known and most successful midnight movies of all time. The quote in this book is from "Fanfare/Don't Dream It, Be It," *The Rocky Horror Picture Show*, 1975.

WILLIAM SHAKESPEARE (4/23/1564–4/23/1616) was an English playwright and poet whose impressive body of work—including approximately thirty-eight plays and 154 sonnets—is widely regarded as the greatest contribution to English literature by a single author. His plays, which include *Hamlet*, *Romeo and Juliet*, *Macbeth*, and *As You Like It*, to name a few, have been performed more than any other playwright's and have made an enduring impression on theater, the arts, poetry, and future generations of writers. The quote in this book is from *Hamlet*, 1599–1601.

AESOP (c. 620–564 BC) was a storyteller in ancient Greece about whom little is known—in fact, there is scant evidence that he actually existed other than being mentioned by Aristotle and Plutarch, among other ancient sources. The fables attributed to Aesop, which are populated with animals that often speak and behave like humans, usually end with a moral meant to teach a lesson. The quote in this book is from *The Lion and the Mouse.*

JANUARY 26: **OSCAR WILDE** (10/16/1854–11/30/1900) was an Irish author, playwright, and poet. Although his best-known works are *The Picture of Dorian Gray* and *The Importance of Being Earnest*, he wrote a collection of stories for children that included "The Happy Prince," "The Nightingale and the Rose," and others.

JANUARY 27: **LUCIUS ANNAEUS SENECA** (c. 4 BC–AD 65), also known as Seneca the Younger, was a Roman philosopher and dramatist, as well as an adviser to Emperor Nero. He was a follower of the Stoic doctrine, a philosophy founded in Athens that espoused the belief that happiness is achieved through leading a simple, virtuous life in harmony with nature.

JANUARY 28: **THE ORACLE OF DELPHI** (c. 1400 BC) was built to honor Delphi, the priestess who served as a seer in the Temple of Apollo at Delphi, which was built near a sacred spring. People from all over Greece would seek answers and listen to the Oracle's prophecies, which were said to come directly from Apollo.

JANUARY 29: **VICTOR HUGO** (2/26/1802–5/22/1885) was one of the most acclaimed French writers of all time. His writings, which included poetry and plays as well as novels such as *Les Misérables* and *The Hunchback of Notre-Dame*, often dealt with themes of social injustice and the plight of the poor. The quotes in this book are from *Les Misérables*, 1862 (January 29 and October 24) and from *Ninety-Three*, 1874 (February 3, March 17, April 28, and October 16).

JANUARY 30: **ELEANOR ROOSEVELT** (10/11/1884–11/7/1962) was the wife of President Franklin D. Roosevelt and served as first lady longer than any other woman in history. She was an outspoken advocate for human rights, championing equal rights for women, as well as being an early supporter of the growing civil rights movement. After her husband's death, she was appointed a delegate to the United Nations, where she helped draft the Universal Declaration of Human Rights.

FEBRUARY 1: **JAMES THURBER** (12/8/1894–11/2/1961) was a popular humorist celebrated for his cartoons and short stories, which were mainly published in the *New Yorker* magazine. His best-known stories include "The Dog That Bit People," "The Night the Bed Fell," and "The Secret Life of Walter Mitty." He is also the author of over seventy-five fables that feature anthropomorphic animals and usually have an underlying moral message. The quote in this book is from "The Scotty Who Knew Too Much," 1939.

FEBRUARY 2: **STEPHEN GRELLET** (11/2/1773–11/16/1855) was a Quaker who became known across North America and many countries in Europe as an advocate of reforming educational policies and improving conditions in hospitals and prisons.

FEBRUARY 3: See **VICTOR HUGO**, January 29

FEBRUARY 5: **ARCHIMEDES** (287–212 BC), also known as Archimedes of Syracuse, was a mathematician, astronomer, physicist, inventor, and engineer in ancient Greece. Among other mathematical achievements, he is credited with creating an accurate approximation of pi and a system of exponentiation to express very large numbers. He is generally considered to be one of the greatest mathematicians of all time.

FEBRUARY 6: **ALICE WALKER** (2/9/1944–present) is an acclaimed novelist, political activist, and winner of the National Book Award and the Pulitzer Prize for Fiction. She is best known for her hugely successful novel *The Color Purple*, which became a bestseller and was later adapted into a critically acclaimed film and Broadway musical. Some of her other works are *Meridian* and *The Third Life of Grange Copeland*. The quotes in this book are from *The Color Purple*, 1982.

FEBRUARY 8: **PABLO PICASSO** (10/25/1881–4/8/1973) was a Spanish painter, sculptor, stage designer, and playwright. He was one of the greatest and most influential artists of the twentieth century. He was a founder of the Cubist movement, with paintings such as *Les Demoiselles d'Avignon* and *Guernica*, which portrayed the horror of the bombing of Guernica during the Spanish Civil War. Other famous works, such as *The Old Guitarist* and *Boy with a Pipe*, are examples of his Blue Period and Rose Period, two of the styles he experimented with over the course of his long life.

FEBRUARY 9: **DANTE ALIGHIERI** (1265–1321) was an Italian poet of the medieval period whose best-known work, *The Divine Comedy*, is a masterpiece of world literature. He is often referred to as the father of the Italian language. *The Divine Comedy* narrates the author's journey through Hell, Purgatory, and Paradise. His guide is Virgil, the author of the *Aeneid*, who died more than a thousand years before him.

FEBRUARY 11: **MICHAEL DANTE DIMARTINO** (10/1/1983–present) and **BRYAN KONIETZKO** (6/1/1975–present) are the creators of the television series *Avatar: The Last Airbender*. Aang is a character from the series who has the unique ability to bend air, water, earth, and fire. The quote in this book is from *Avatar: The Last Airbender*, 2006.

FEBRUARY 12: **CLAUDE BERNARD** (7/12/1813–2/10/1878) was a French physiologist who is credited with helping to establish a principle of the scientific method: the use of blind experiments to ensure objectivity. He coined the term "homeostasis" when he introduced the concept that the internal environments of organisms self-regulate vital processes. The quote in this book is from *Bulletin of the New York Academy of Medicine*, Vol. IV, 1928.

FEBRUARY 14: **OVID** (3/20/43 BC–AD 17), one of the three great poets of Latin literature (along with Virgil and Horace), wrote *Metamorphoses*, an epic poem spanning fifteen books that narrates the history of the world. Most of the "history" is based on classical Greek myths, so *Metamorphoses* is filled with stories of gods and goddesses, heroes, and magical beasts. Ovid's works influenced many great poets that came after him, such as Dante and Shakespeare.

FEBRUARY 15: **VICTOR BORGE** (1/3/1909–12/23/2000), also known as the Clown Prince of Denmark, was a Danish comedian, conductor, and pianist. He performed as a classical concert pianist and also as a comedian in Europe until the Nazis occupied Denmark during World War II. He immigrated to America, becoming very popular as a radio personality and later hosting his own television show, *The Victor Borge Show*. The quote in this book is from *Smilet er den korteste afstand*, 1997.

FEBRUARY 16: **LLOYD JONES** (3/23/1955–present) is an author from New Zealand whose books include *Biografi*, *Here at the End of the World We Learn to Dance*, and *Mister Pip*, which won the Commonwealth Writers Prize and was shortlisted for the Booker Prize.

FEBRUARY 18: **AUGUSTE RODIN** (11/12/1840–11/17/1917) was a French sculptor whose work, known for its realistic depiction of the human body and form, established him as one of the greatest sculptors of all time. His best-known works, *The Thinker* and *The Kiss*, are two of the most widely recognized works of art. The quote in this book is from *The Origins of Creativity*, 1964.

FEBRUARY 19: **NELSON MANDELA** (7/18/1918–12/5/2013) was a South African anti-apartheid revolutionary who served as the president of South Africa from 1994 to 1999, winning the country's first fully representative democratic election only four years after his twenty-seven-year-long incarceration for anti-government activities. He is internationally recognized for his life's work to abolish the institutionalized racism, poverty, and inequality of apartheid. The quote on this date is from *Long Walk to Freedom*, 1995.

FEBRUARY 20: **ABRAHAM LINCOLN** (12/12/1809–4/15/1865) was the sixteenth president of the United States. Having declared his intention to abolish slavery, he was elected in 1860 and reacted quickly to the pro-slavery states that had moved to secede from the Union. He led the country through the Civil War until his assassination in April 1865. Lincoln gave many powerful speeches that are often quoted today.

FEBRUARY 21: **BOB MERRILL** (5/17/1921–2/17/1998) and **JULE STYNE** (12/31/1905–9/20/1994) were the lyricists of the song "Don't Rain on My Parade," which appeared in the film *Funny Girl*, starring a young Barbra Streisand. The quote in this book is from "Don't Rain on My Parade," in *Funny Girl*, 1964.

FEBRUARY 22: **MENCIUS** (372–289 BC) was an ancient Chinese philosopher in the Confucian tradition. He was a pupil of Confucius's grandson Zisi and traveled throughout China for forty years to offer advice to rulers. Mencius believed that people were innately good and that society's influence was to blame for bad moral character.

FEBRUARY 25: **SIR PHILIP SIDNEY** (11/30/1554–11/17/1586) was an English poet, scholar, and soldier during the reign of Queen Elizabeth. He is best known for his work *The Defence of Poesie*, but he also wrote *Astrophil and Stella* and *The Countess of Pembroke's Arcadia*. He was a proponent of the Protestant movement in England and Europe and died from wounds suffered in battle against the Spaniards at the age of thirty-one. The quote in this book is from *An Apology of Poetry, or The Defence of Poesie*, 1582.

FEBRUARY 26: **THOMAS JEFFERSON** (4/13/1743–7/4/1826) was the third president of the United States. Chief author of the Declaration of Independence, he was one of the country's Founding Fathers and was a member of the First Continental Congress. During his presidential terms (1801–1809), he oversaw the acquisition of the Louisiana Territory from France and appointed Lewis and Clark to explore the newly acquired territories. He was a polymath, designing his plantation in Monticello while also being a prolific writer and champion of Enlightenment ideals. He believed in the ability of science and discovery to elevate the human condition.

FEBRUARY 27: **EPICTETUS** (AD 55–135) was a Greek philosopher who believed that while the lives of humans are controlled by fate, we can still choose between doing good and doing evil, which can determine our own fates. He believed that individuals could take ownership for their actions through self-examination, discipline, and leading a pure and simple life.

FEBRUARY 28: **SOPHOCLES** (496–406 BC) was a Greek playwright, best known for his tragedies *Oedipus the King, Electra,* and *Antigone.* His work had a profound influence on literature, both as dramas and as poetry, and are still staged today, almost three thousand years after they were written.

FEBRUARY 29: **DAWN LAFFERTY HOCHSPRUNG** (1965–12/14/2012) was the principal of Sandy Hook Elementary School in Newtown, Connecticut. On December 14, 2012, she and twenty-five others were victims of a school shooting. The tragedy inspired the creation of the Dawn Lafferty Hochsprung Center for the Promotion of Mental Health and School Safety, which seeks to create safe school environments and support the mental health of every child.

MARCH 1: **BLAISE PASCAL** (6/19/1623–8/19/1662) was a French mathematician, physicist, inventor, and author who is credited with inventing the world's first calculator, as well as making numerous discoveries in mathematics, geometry, and the physical sciences. He also left behind his numerous writings on philosophy, including *Pensées,* which is considered to be a masterpiece of theological narrative.

MARCH 2: **MARGARET MEAD** (12/16/1901–11/15/1978) was an American anthropologist whose studies of "primitive" societies in Samoa and the South Pacific led to a greater understanding of sexuality and race in Western culture.

MARCH 3: **WALT WHITMAN** (5/31/1819–3/26/1892) was one of the greatest American poets of the nineteenth century. Best remembered for *Leaves of Grass,* which was praised by his contemporaries Emerson and Thoreau, the work was panned by critics for its use of prose and "obscene" themes. Unable to sustain himself as a poet, Whitman was also a journalist and editor, and helped support the Union during the Civil War by volunteering as a nurse in army hospitals.

MARCH 4: **THOMAS TRAHERNE** (1636–9/27/1674) was an English clergyman whose poetry was only discovered and published more than two hundred years after his death. Best remembered for *Centuries of Meditations*, which is a collection of short reflections on Christian life and philosophy, his writings influenced future poets, such as Elizabeth Jennings and C. S. Lewis, the author of the Chronicles of Narnia.

MARCH 6: **ST. BASIL OF CAESAREA** (AD 330–379), also known as St. Basil the Great, was a Greek bishop in the country that is now Turkey. He was an important religious and political figure who was known for his service to the poor and underprivileged.

MARCH 7: **RALPH WALDO EMERSON** (5/25/1803–4/27/1882) was an American writer who was a leader in the Transcendentalist movement, which believed in the inherent goodness of people, and that nature— not organized religion or institutions—was the key to self-knowledge and independence. He is best known for his essays "Nature" and "Self-Reliance," but he also wrote "The Over-Soul," "Circles," "The Poet," and "Experience."

MARCH 8: **MARTIN H. FISCHER** (11/10/1879–1/19/1962) was a physician and author whose notes about the practice of medicine have been seminal to the education of aspiring doctors for over fifty years.

MARCH 9: **CONFUCIUS** (551–479 BC) was a Chinese philosopher whose teachings about compassion, benevolence, and kindness are still followed today. The primary focus of his ideology is Rén, or "loving others," which he considered the key to living a good and honest life. He was the first to use what has come to be called the Golden Rule: "What you do not wish for yourself, do not do to others."

MARCH 10: **DALAI LAMA**, born Tenzin Gyatso (7/6/1935–present), is the spiritual leader of Tibetan Buddhists and a symbol of kindness for people around the world. He has stated that his life is guided by three major commitments: the promotion of basic human values or secular ethics in the interest of human happiness, the fostering of inter-religious harmony, and the preservation of Tibet's Buddhist culture, a culture of peace and nonviolence. The quote in this book (on November 11) is from *Kindness, Clarity, and Insight*, 1984.

MARCH 11: See **MARK TWAIN**, January 7

MARCH 12: **EMILY DICKINSON** (12/10/1830–5/15/1886) was an American poet from Amherst, Massachusetts. She led a very reclusive and quiet life, seldom leaving the house she grew up in and counting her siblings as her closest friends. Her family found forty hand-bound books containing over 1,600 poems after she died, which were then published. She remains one of the most beloved poets of our time. The quote in this book is from "That Love is all there is."

MARCH 13: **HENRY STANLEY HASKINS** (1875–1957) was an American financier whose observations, published anonymously in 1940 in a book called *Meditations in Wall Street*, were widely read. It wasn't until seven years after it was published, though, that Haskins was credited with authorship.

MARCH 14: **BUKKYO DENDO KYOKAI (BDK)** is the Society for the Promotion of Buddhism, which is dedicated to the teachings of Buddha. Under the direction of the Reverend Dr. Yehan Numata, the BDK assembled a team of Japanese scholars to edit a new edition of *The Teaching of Buddha*, which presents an easy-to-understand introduction to Buddhism, as well as a history. This book can be found in most hotel rooms in Japan.

MARCH 15: **VOLTAIRE**, born François-Marie Arouet (11/21/1694–5/30/1778), was a French writer who became one of the major voices of the Enlightenment. His body of writings, which include plays, poems, and essays on history and philosophy, were often satirical in nature, attacking both the monarchy and the church—for which he was exiled several times in his lifetime. He believed in religious freedom and tolerance, and advocated for the separation of church and state. The quotes in this book are from "Le Mondain," 1736 (March 15); and from "Deuxième discours: de la liberté," *Sept discours en vers sur l'homme*, 1738.

MARCH 16: **PIERRE CARLET DE CHAMBLAIN DE MARIVAUX** (2/4/1688–2/12/1763)—a contemporary of Voltaire—was a French writer and dramatist whose work, especially comedies such as *Le triomphe de l'amour (The Triumph of Love)*, *Le jeu de l'amour et du hasard (The Game of Love and Chance)*, and *Les fausses confidences (False Admissions)*, was widely known in France.

MARCH 17: See **VICTOR HUGO**, January 29

MARCH 20: **MOTHER TERESA** (8/26/1910–9/5/1997) was a Roman Catholic missionary who was honored with the Nobel Peace Prize in 1979 for her humanitarian work in India. She founded the organization called Missionaries of Charity, which currently consists of over 4,500 nuns in 133 different countries. This organization runs soup kitchens, orphanages, schools, counseling programs, and homes for people with HIV/AIDS, leprosy, and tuberculosis.

MARCH 23: **JEAN-JACQUES ROUSSEAU** (6/28/1712–7/2/1778) was a Swiss writer whose works were highly influential in their time. His novel *Julie, or the New Heloise*, became wildly popular immediately upon publication, and his nonfiction work *Emile, or On Education*, about the relationship between society and the individual, espoused principles that aligned with the architects of the French Revolution. Rousseau believed that human beings are born good, and that the power to make laws should be in the hands of the people.

MARCH 26: See **DALAI LAMA**, March 10

MARCH 27: **JOHANN WOLFGANG VON GOETHE** (8/28/1749–3/22/1832) is one of the greatest and most influential German authors of all time. His first novel, *The Sorrows of Young Werther*, made him a celebrity at the age of twenty-five. Other works, such as *Faust*, as well as his poetry and maxims, inspired artists, writers, and composers for decades to come.

MARCH 28: **GEORGES JACQUES** Danton (10/26/1759–4/5/1794) was one of the leaders of the French Revolution and a key figure in the overthrow of the monarchy. A lawyer and brilliant orator, he became critical of the reign of terror that followed the revolution, and for those moderate views—especially his opposition to Robespierre—he was guillotined.

MARCH 29: **WILLIAM BLAKE** (11/28/1757–8/12/1827) was an English artist and poet whose work, rich in mystical language and ideas about the nature of man, influenced the poetry and art of the Romantic movement, the Pre-Raphaelites, and, hundreds of years later, the Beat poets. His books, including his best-known works, *Songs of Innocence* and *Songs of Experience*, both of which he illustrated, are full of religious and mythological symbolism. The quote in this book is from *The Marriage of Heaven and Hell*, 1790–93.

MARCH 30: **RuPAUL (ANDRE CHARLES)** (11/17/1960–present) is an American television and recording artist originally from California. Having achieved recognition as a drag queen, RuPaul recorded a hit song in 1992,

"Supermodel (You Better Work)," and has hosted a number of television shows since.

APRIL 1: **SAPPHO** (c. 610–c. 570 BC) was a Greek lyric poet widely regarded as one of the greatest of world literature, though much of her work has not survived. What work does survive is known for its themes of love and passion.

APRIL 2: **RICHARD HENRY HENGIST HORNE** (12/31/1802–3/13/1884) was an English poet who is best known for the epic poem *Orion*. He was a friend of Elizabeth Barrett Browning and an editor of Charles Dickens's weekly magazine *Household Words*. The quote in this book is from *Orion*, 1843.

APRIL 3: **DANIEL WEBSTER** (1/18/1782–10/24/1852) was a Massachusetts lawyer and U.S. senator who also served as U.S. secretary of state from 1841 to 1843 and again from 1850 to 1852. Well known for his powerful oratory on behalf of American nationalism, he spoke against the expansion of slavery into new territories but also, in an effort to preserve the Union, supported stricter laws for the recovery of runaway slaves. The quote in this book is from an address on laying the cornerstone of the Bunker Hill Monument, 1825.

APRIL 4: **LEO TOLSTOY** (9/9/1828–11/20/1910), aka Count Lev Nikolayevich Tolstoy, was a Russian novelist best known for *War and Peace*, considered by many to be the greatest novel of all time. Born to nobility, Tolstoy spent much of his youth gambling and squandering his family fortune but had a series of spiritual awakenings that led him to espouse an ascetic, almost monastic life in his later years. *Anna Karenina, The Death of Ivan Ilyich,* and many of his other works had a profound influence on pacifists like Gandhi and Martin Luther King, Jr.

APRIL 6: **MAHATMA GANDHI** (10/2/1869–1/30/1948) was a civil rights activist who led India's effort to achieve independence from Britain using nonviolent civil disobedience. He lived modestly and inspired many other civil rights leaders to adopt a strategy of passive resistance.

APRIL 7: **SØREN KIERKEGAARD** (5/5/1813–11/11/1855) was a Danish philosopher and theologian whose work inspired the existentialist movement. He wrote about organized religion and morality, specifically about the individual's responsibility to become a good human being. The quote in this book is from Journals, IV A 164, 1843.

APRIL 8: **HENRY DAVID THOREAU** (7/12/1817–5/6/1862) was a writer, philosopher, and naturalist whose greatest work, *Walden,* illustrated his passion for simple living in nature. He was part of the Transcendentalist movement and, in keeping with his beliefs, lived for two years in a hut he built himself near Walden Pond. He was an abolitionist and believed in the inherent goodness of people. The quotes in this book are both from *Walden,* 1854.

APRIL 9: **JAMES RUSSELL LOWELL** (2/22/1819–8/12/1891) was an American Romantic poet who worked to end slavery by editing an abolitionist newspaper, *The Atlantic Monthly,* which later became known as *The Atlantic* and is still in publication today. The quote in this book is from *Sonnets,* 1844

APRIL 10: **JONATHAN SWIFT** (11/30/1667–10/19/1745) was an Irish writer who is best remembered for his work *Gulliver's Travels,* the satirical account of a man's journey through fictional lands—which was also a critical exploration of modern English ways and Enlightenment thinking. The quote in this book is from *Polite Conversation,* 1738.

APRIL 11: **VINCE LOMBARDI** (6/11/1913–9/3/1970) is considered one of the greatest coaches in NFL history for leading the Green Bay Packers to five championships in seven years. He was born in Brooklyn, New York, and played college and semi-professional football before beginning his illustrious coaching career as an assistant at Fordham University and with the New York Giants.

APRIL 12: **WILLIAM MAKEPEACE THACKERAY** (7/18/1811–12/24/1863) was an English novelist who during his lifetime was as famous and widely read as Charles Dickens. He is best known for *Vanity Fair,* a satire of English society; *The History of Henry Esmond, Esq.;* and *The Virginians.*

APRIL 14: **JIMMY (JAMES WILLIAM) JOHNSON** (7/16/1943–present) is an American football broadcaster and analyst and was also a player and coach. He coached the Dallas Cowboys to two consecutive Super Bowl wins and was inducted into the College Football Hall of Fame as a coach in 2012.

APRIL 15: **EDWARD EVERETT HALE** (4/3/1822–6/10/1909) was an author of numerous works, including biographies and histories, but is most remembered for his novel *The Man Without a Country.* He was an abolitionist, a minister in the Unitarian church, an advocate for education, and a founder of the Lend a Hand Society, which inspired countless philanthropic organizations and works.

APRIL 16: **TOM WILSON** (8/1/1931–9/16/2011) was an American cartoonist best known for creating the character of Ziggy in 1969. Ziggy is a small, iconic figure (most remembered for his protuberant nose) who has an array of pets, including a dog, a cat, a fish, and a duck.

APRIL 17: **HENRY VAN DYKE** (11/10/1852–4/10/1933) was an American author, teacher, and minister whose literary works were often about nature and religion. Known for his sermons, which preached tolerance and altruism, he was appointed ambassador to the Netherlands and Luxembourg by President Woodrow Wilson, a friend and former classmate. The quote in this book is from the Handicapped Individuals Services and Training Act in a hearing before the Subcommittee on Select Education of the Committee on Education and Labor, House of Representatives, on September 2, 1982.

APRIL 18: **JOSEPH CAMPBELL** (3/26/1904–10/30/1987) was an American scholar and teacher best known for his work in comparative mythology and for his theory of the hero's journey, which finds a common pattern in all the world's mythic narratives and creation stories.

APRIL 20: **JOSEPH NORRIS** (1699–1733) was an American poet who wrote verse, devotional poetry, and essays on church history and doctrine.

APRIL 21: **ROBERT FROST** (3/26/1874–1/29/1963) was one of the greatest American poets of the twentieth century. He was awarded four Pulitzer Prizes over the course of his long life. He often wrote about rural life in New England and is best known for his poem "The Road Not Taken." The quote in this book is from "Hyla Brook," 1920.

APRIL 22: **CARL SCHURZ** (3/2/1829–5/14/1906) was an editor, politician, writer, and teacher who was forced to flee Germany in his youth when he took part in the German revolutionary movement. After arriving in the United States, he became a lawyer, was a brigadier general of volunteers in the Union Army during the Civil War, and served as a U.S. senator. The quote in this book is from an address at Faneuil Hall, Boston, on April 18, 1859.

APRIL 23: **ALBERT SCHWEITZER** (1/14/1875–9/4/1965) was a philosopher, physician, and concert organist known for his historical work on Jesus. He worked in Africa as a medical missionary, founding a hospital there before becoming a prisoner of war during World War I. He won the Nobel Peace Prize in 1952 for his philanthropy.

APRIL 24: **PEARL S. BUCK** (6/26/1892–3/6/1973) was an American author best known for her book *The Good Earth,* which won the Nobel Prize in Literature for 1938. She was raised in China by missionary parents, and most of her work is about the interplay between the East and the West. The quote in this book is from the *This I Believe* radio broadcast, 1951.

APRIL 25: **KARLE WILSON BAKER** (10/13/1878–11/9/1960) was an American writer from Texas who was nominated for the Pulitzer Prize for Poetry in 1931 for her work *Dreamers on Horseback.* She also wrote the *Texas Flag Primer,* a history of Texas that was taught in many public schools. The quote in this book is from "Good Company."

APRIL 26: See **MENCIUS**, February 22

APRIL 27: **WILLIAM JAMES** (1/11/1842–8/26/1910) was an American philosopher who was instrumental in establishing psychology—or the "study of the soul"—as its own empirical science, separate and distinct from philosophy. He was closely associated with the philosophical tradition of pragmatism.

APRIL 28: See **VICTOR HUGO**, January 29

APRIL 29: **AUSTIN KLEON** (6/16/1983–present) is a *New York Times* bestselling author of three illustrated books: *Steal Like an Artist, Show Your Work!,* and *Newspaper Blackout.* He has spoken about creativity at organizations like Pixar, Google, and TEDx. He lives in Austin, Texas. The quotes in this book are from *Steal Like an Artist,* 2012.

MAY 1: **GRANDMA NELLY** is the fictional grandmother of Mr. Browne, whom he quotes in *365 Days of Wonder: Mr. Browne's Book of Precepts,* by R. J. Palacio. The character, and the precept itself, are based on R. J. Palacio's own mother.

MAY 2: **JOHN WESLEY** (6/28/1703–3/2/1791) was an English Anglican minister who was a cofounder of the Methodist Church. Under Wesley's guidance, Methodists became known as the leaders in many social causes, such as prison reform and abolition.

MAY 3: **HAN SUYIN** (9/12/1917–11/2/2012) was best known for writing *A Many-Splendored Thing*, a popular novel that was made into a film in 1955. The daughter of a Chinese father and Belgian mother, she grew up in China but wrote primarily in English and French. Her novels, set in modern China, show her support of the Chinese Communist revolution.

MAY 4: **FATHER (FREDERICK WILLIAM) FABER** (6/28/1814–9/26/1863) was an English Catholic priest in the 1800s. He is best known for writing several hymns, the most famous of which is "Faith of Our Fathers."

MAY 5: See **VINCE LOMBARDI**, April 11

MAY 6: **CHUANG TZU** (369–286 BC), or Zhuangzi, a defining figure in Taoism, is best known for writing the *Zhuangzi*, a collection of stories illustrating how to live in harmony with the Tao through meditation, moderation, compassion, humility, and oneness with nature.

MAY 8: **C. S. (CLIVE STAPLETON) LEWIS** (11/29/1898–11/22/1963) was an Irish-born writer best known for his series of children's books, the Chronicles of Narnia. A devout Christian, Lewis held academic positions at Cambridge University and Oxford University, where he became close friends with fellow novelist J.R.R. Tolkien.

MAY 9: See **RALPH WALDO EMERSON**, March 7

MAY 10: **JALAL AD-DIN MUHAMMAD RUMI** (9/30/1207–12/17/1273), known as Rumi, was a thirteenth-century Persian-language poet and Sufi mystic whose work has been widely translated. Much of his poetry is devoted to the idea of restoring oneness with God.

MAY 12: **J. R. (JAMES RUSSELL) MILLER** (3/20/1840–7/2/1912) was an American author of highly popular Christian-themed literature, including *The Beauty of Kindness*, which was published in 1905. He was a member of the United Presbyterian Church and pastored several churches in Pennsylvania and Illinois.

MAY 13: **HELEN KELLER** (6/27/1880–6/1/1968) was a lecturer, author, and political activist. At nineteen months old, she was struck blind and deaf after a bout with either meningitis or scarlet fever, and she was unable to communicate throughout her early childhood. Her parents found a young tutor by the name of Anne Sullivan when Helen was six years old, and through perseverance, Anne was able to teach Helen how to communicate using her fingers. Helen eventually mastered several forms of communication, graduated from college, and became an advocate for the blind, women's suffrage, and labor rights.

MAY 15: **MIA FARROW** (2/9/1945–present) is an actress and activist who starred in twelve of Woody Allen's films. She is also famous for her roles in the films *The Great Gatsby* and *Rosemary's Baby*. The quote in this book is from an interview in *Esquire* called "Mia Farrow: What I've Learned," June 2006.

MAY 17: **JONATHAN WINTERS** (11/11/1925–4/11/2013) was an American comedian known for his comedy albums and appearances in many films and countless television shows.

MAY 18: **JOHN LENNON** (10/9/1940–12/8/1980) was a member of the legendary English rock band the Beatles, which was founded by him and fellow band member Paul McCartney. The two became a prolific songwriting team, writing over 180 songs—many of which are the most recognizable songs of our time, such as "Yellow Submarine," "Penny Lane," and "Eleanor Rigby." During his time with the Beatles, and after he went solo in 1970, Lennon was known for his political activism and his opposition to war. The quote in this book is from "Give Peace a Chance," 1969.

MAY 19: **ROBERT BYRNE** (5/22/1930–present) is an author and billiards instructor, best known beyond the sports world for his collections of humorous quotations, including *The 637 Best Things Anybody Ever Said*, published in 1983.

MAY 20: **W.E.B. (WILLIAM EDWARDS BURGHARDT) DU BOIS** (2/23/1868–8/27/1963) was an African American author, teacher, and civil rights activist, and one of the cofounders of the National Association for the Advancement of Colored People (NAACP). He was the first African American to earn a doctorate from Harvard University, and through his writings and lectures was able to advocate for policies to end lynching, discrimination in education and employment, and the Jim Crow laws. He wrote numerous books, and his best known is *The Souls of Black Folk*. The quote in this book is from his "last message to the world," read at his funeral, written 1957.

MAY 23: **MARCUS AURELIUS** (AD 121–180) was a Roman emperor who ruled from 161 to 180. His most famous work is *Meditations*, a book that exemplified his belief in stoicism, or the idea that virtue, embodied by self-control, is the key to happiness.

MAY 24: **PYTHAGORAS** (570–495 BC) was a Greek philosopher best known for his work in mathematics, science, and geometry, including the Pythagorean Theorem, which can be written as the equation $a^2 + b^2 = c^2$.

MAY 25: **DESIDERIUS ERASMUS** (10/27/1466–7/12/1536) was a Dutch philosopher, humanist, and teacher. He published a new Latin and Greek edition of the New Testament, and he also wrote *On Free Will*, *The Praise of Folly*, and *The Handbook of a Christian Soldier*.

MAY 29: See **MARK TWAIN**, January 7

MAY 30: **MATTHEW ARNOLD** (12/24/1822–4/15/1888) was an English poet of the Victorian age, as well as a literary critic. His *Essays in Criticism* is one of the most popular treatises on literary criticism to this day. The quote in this book is from "From the Hymn of Empedocles," in *Empedocles on Etna*, 1852.

MAY 31: **CHARLES BAUDELAIRE** (4/9/1821–8/31/1867) was one of the great French poets of the nineteenth century, best known for his work "Les fleurs du mal," translated as "The Flowers of Evil." He is credited with coining the literary term "modernity" to convey the rejection of tradition in favor of individualism and equality.

JUNE 1: **THE POLYPHONIC SPREE** is a choral rock group whose music is characterized by its psychedelic pop and symphonic rock sound. It was founded in 2000 by lead singer Tim DeLaughter (11/18/1965–present). The quote in this book is from "Light and Day/Reach for the Sun," 2003.

JUNE 3: **ST. FRANCIS OF ASSISI** (1181–10/3/1226) was a Catholic friar who gave up his life of wealth and privilege to serve the poor in the name of Christ. He is known as the patron saint of animals because of his love for nature, which he believed reflected the nature of God. He founded the Franciscan Order.

JUNE 4: **BOB MARLEY** (2/6/1945–5/11/1981) was a Jamaican reggae singer and songwriter who became one of the world's bestselling artists of all time. A follower of the Rastafari movement, Marley infused his music with his spiritual beliefs, rejecting materialism and fighting oppression. The quote in this book is from "Three Little Birds," 1977.

JUNE 6: **RICHARD RODGERS** (6/28/1902–12/30/1979) and **OSCAR HAMMERSTEIN** (7/12/1895–8/23/1960) were the songwriting team responsible for some of the greatest Broadway musicals of the twentieth century, including *The King and I, Oklahoma!, South Pacific, Carousel,* and *The Sound of Music.* The quote in this book is from "Climb Ev'ry Mountain," *The Sound of Music,* 1959.

JUNE 7: **CHARLES CARROLL** (9/19/1737–11/14/1832) was one of the original signers of the Declaration of Independence. A Maryland senator from 1789 to 1792, he was an early advocate for separation from Great Britain.

JUNE 8: See **RALPH WALDO EMERSON**, March 7

JUNE 9: **LEWIS CARROLL** (1/27/1832–1/14/1898), born Charles Dodgson, was an English writer best known for his successful children's works: *Alice's Adventures in Wonderland, Through the Looking-Glass,* and the poem "Jabberwocky." He was also a mathematician of great renown and a brilliant amateur photographer.

JUNE 10: **HENRY FORD** (7/30/1863–4/7/1947) was the founder of the Ford Motor Company, a large automaker still in operation in Michigan. Through the development of the assembly line technique of mass production, he was able to manufacture the Model T automobile so that it would be "a motorcar for the great multitude," not just the wealthy.

JUNE 12: **ALBERT EINSTEIN** (3/14/1879–4/18/1955) was a German physicist whose theory of relativity has become the basis of all modern science. He is best known for his famous equation $E = mc^2$. Einstein was awarded the Nobel Prize in Physics in 1921 for his discovery of the law of the photoelectric effect, which was a key finding in the development of quantum theory. In addition to his scientific work, Einstein was a great champion for civil rights. The quote in this book is from *Mein Weltbild (My Worldview)*, 1931.

JUNE 14: See **MAHATMA GANDHI**, April 6

JUNE 15: **JOHANNES KEPLER** (12/27/1571–11/15/1630) was a German scientist who discovered the laws of planetary motion, which stated that the planets—including Earth—moved in orbits around the sun. His work deeply influenced Isaac Newton's law of universal gravitation.

JUNE 18: **DENIS DIDEROT** (10/5/1713–7/31/1784) was a French writer and philosopher of the Enlightenment. He cofounded *Encyclopédie*—the first of its kind to be made up of contributions from different authors—which was an attempt by its founders to gather all the knowledge of the world in one place.

JUNE 19: **RABINDRANATH TAGORE** (5/7/1861–8/7/1941) was a Bengali poet and writer who won the Nobel Prize in Literature in 1913. Although he was knighted by the British in 1915, he renounced that honor in protest of British rule and became an outspoken supporter of Indian independence.

JUNE 20: **VIOLETA PARRA** (10/4/1917–2/5/1967) was a folklorist, ethnomusicologist, songwriter, and composer from Chile who is best known for her song "Gracias a la Vida." The quote in this book is from "Gracias a la Vida," 1966.

JUNE 21: **MICHELANGELO BUONARROTI** (3/6/1475–2/18/1564) is considered one of the greatest artists of all time. He was a sculptor, painter, and architect. His gargantuan frescoes on the ceiling of the Sistine Chapel in Rome, as well as *The Last Judgment* on the altar wall, are among the most famous works of art in history. His sculpture *David,* which stands in the Galleria dell'Accademia in Florence, is one of the most recognizable sculptures in the world.

JUNE 23: See **J.R.R. TOLKIEN**, January 17

JUNE 24: **ÉMILE COUÉ** (2/26/1857–7/2/1926) was a French pharmacist who was one of the first proponents of the use of psychotherapy. His autosuggestion, or self-hypnosis, method uses the mantra "Every day, in every way, I am getting better and better" as a way of achieving general well-being and good health.

JUNE 27: **WILLIAM MORRIS** (3/24/1834–10/3/1896) was an English textile designer closely associated with the British Arts and Crafts Movement. He was also a poet, novelist, and social activist.

JUNE 28: **PLINY THE ELDER** (AD 23–8/25/79) was a Roman philosopher whose last work, *Naturalis Historia,* became the model for all other encyclopedias. He died while attempting to flee the erupting volcano in Pompeii.

JUNE 29: See **KAHLIL GIBRAN**, January 9

JULY 1: **ANNE HERBERT** (1952–present) is an American writer and editor. She is the author of *Random Kindness and Senseless Acts of Beauty,* among other things. The quote in this book is from *Whole Earth Review,* "Handy Tips on How to Behave at the Death of the World," Spring 1995.

JULY 2: **DAVID LLOYD** George (1/17/1863–3/26/1945) was a British politician and prime minister of England during and immediately after World War I. He attended the Paris Peace Conference of 1919, which partitioned Europe after the German defeat.

JULY 3: **ALFRED ADLER** (2/7/1870–5/28/1937) was an Austrian psychotherapist and medical doctor who founded the concept of individual psychology. He coined the phrase "inferiority complex," which revealed the role that feelings of inferiority play in the development of personality. The quote in this book is from *Problems of Neurosis: A Book of Case Histories,* 1929.

JULY 4: **SAMUEL JOHNSON** (9/18/1709–12/13/1784) was an English writer whose dictionary, *A Dictionary of the English Language,* was the foremost in Britain for 150 years until it was supplanted by the *Oxford English Dictionary.* He is also the subject of one of the most well-known biographies, *Life of Samuel Johnson.*

JULY 5: **LES BROWN** (2/17/1945–present) is a motivational speaker who encourages people with his own story of success, despite the lack of opportunities he was afforded as a child. He inspires audiences to "step beyond their limitations and into their greatness."

JULY 7: **HENRY WARD BEECHER** (6/24/1813–3/8/1887) was an American clergyman and ardent abolitionist. He was the first pastor of the Plymouth Church in Brooklyn, New York, where he gained recognition for his outspoken sermons in which he preached the "Gospel of Love," which emphasized God's love and rejected the notion of Hell. His sister Harriet Beecher Stowe attained international fame with her abolitionist novel *Uncle Tom's Cabin.*

JULY 8: **SIR JAMES MATTHEW BARRIE** (5/9/1860–6/19/1937), also known as J. M. Barrie, was a Scottish novelist and playwright, best remembered for his play *Peter Pan,* which he turned into a novel in 1911, about a mischievous boy named Peter Pan who lives in a magical realm called Neverland.

JULY 9: **GAUTAMA BUDDHA** (563–483 BC), also known as Siddhartha or simply as Buddha, was a spiritual leader whose life and teachings inspired Buddhism. Buddha, which means "awakened one" or "enlightened one," was believed to have lived in eastern India. He spoke of the "Four Noble Truths" that are needed to achieve a state of Nirvana, or spiritual bliss, and to be free from ignorance and hatred.

JULY 10: **ALDOUS HUXLEY** (7/26/1894–11/22/1963) was a British author best known for his dystopian masterpiece, *Brave New World*, which is widely considered one of the greatest novels of the English language. It tells the story of a world in the future in which natural reproduction no longer exists and individuality, along with critical thinking, has been stamped out. The quote in this book is from *Time Must Have a Stop*, 1944.

JULY 13: **IRVING STONE** (7/14/1903–7/26/1989) was an American author best known for his epic biographical novels on famous artists, such as *The Agony and the Ecstasy*, which is about Michelangelo, and *Lust for Life*, about Vincent van Gogh.

JULY 14: **MIGUEL DE CERVANTES** (9/29/1547–4/22/1616) was a Spanish writer whose masterpiece, *Don Quixote*, is widely considered to be the greatest work of Spanish literature. It has inspired countless authors and artists over the centuries, including the 1965 Broadway musical *Man of La Mancha*.

JULY 15: **ANTHONY ROBBINS** (2/29/1960–present) is a self-help author, motivational speaker, and life coach who is best known for his book *Unlimited Power*.

JULY 16: **MARTIN CHARNIN** (11/24/1934–present) is the creator and director of *Annie*, a Broadway musical based on the Harold Gray comic strip *Little Orphan Annie*, about a curly-red-haired orphan named Annie; her dog, Sandy; and a billionaire businessman, named Daddy Warbucks, who eventually adopts her. The quote in this book is from "Tomorrow" in *Annie*, 1977.

JULY 17: **CHARLES DICKENS** (2/7/1812–6/9/1870) was a British novelist whose works, such as *A Christmas Carol*, *A Tale of Two Cities*, and *Oliver Twist*, are among the most read and lauded books in the English language. His novels, which were often about disadvantaged characters living in poor conditions, highlighted the need for social reform and an end to class repression. The quote in this book is from *David Copperfield*, 1850.

JULY 18: **GINNY MOORE** (present) is the author of *Don't Make Lemonade: Leaning into Life's Difficult Transitions*. In her book, she encourages readers to face difficulties and changes in life by learning how to process emotions well. She also practices caregiving with an organization called With A Little Help, which she considers a spiritual act.

JULY 19: **JOHN MILTON** (12/9/1608–11/8/1674) was an English poet who lived during a time of political turbulence after the English civil war, the execution of King Charles I, and the Restoration. He believed in the idea of England as a republic, without a king, and supported Oliver Cromwell's rule over the Commonwealth. Best known for his epic poem *Paradise Lost*, a retelling of the biblical story of the Fall of Man, which he wrote late in his life after becoming blind, Milton is now regarded as one of the greatest English poets of all time. The quote in this book is from *Lycidas*, 1637.

JULY 21: **WAYNE GRETZKY** (1/26/1961–present) is a Canadian hockey player who is considered to be the greatest player in his sport. With numerous championships and awards to his name, he was immediately inducted into the Hockey Hall of Fame following his retirement in 1999.

JULY 22: **SCOTT ADAMS** (6/8/1957–present) is an American cartoonist best known for creating the comic strip *Dilbert*, which satirizes office life in large corporations.

JULY 24: **THEODORE ROOSEVELT** (10/27/1858–1/6/1919) became the twenty-sixth American president after the assassination of William McKinley in 1901. He was known for his foreign policy, which included helping Panama become independent from Colombia in exchange for the Panama Canal, and initiated numerous efforts to preserve the natural resources of the United States, including protecting the national parks and expanding national forests.

JULY 25: **JAMES MICHENER** (2/3/1907–10/16/1997) was a prolific American novelist whose books were typically grand, epic multi-generational narratives about the history of different regions of the world. He was awarded the Pulitzer Prize for Fiction in 1948 for *Tales of the South Pacific*. Other works include *Centennial*, *Hawaii*, and *The Drifters*, to name a few. The quote in this book is from *Space*, 1982.

JULY 26: **JOHN RUSKIN** (2/8/1819–1/20/1900) was an English writer, art critic, and philanthropist in the Victorian era. His work reflected his ideas about the role of art and nature in society, seeking to promote the concept of a "social economy." The quote in this book is from *Unto This Last*, 1860.

JULY 27: **MIKE DITKA** (10/18/1939–present) was a professional football player and coach who played with the Chicago Bears in the 1960s and then became their coach in the 1980s. He was inducted into the Hall of Fame for both the NFL and college football.

JULY 29: See **CARL SAGAN**, January 8

JULY 30: See **J. M. BARRIE**, July 8

JULY 31: **E. M. (EDWARD MORGAN) FORSTER** (1/1/1879–6/7/1970) was the English author of *Howards End*, *A Passage to India*, and *A Room with a View*, among other classics. His books often dealt with the struggle between nature and technology, and the importance of kindness and goodwill in maintaining a good and just modern society. He was nominated for the Nobel Prize in Literature thirteen times, but never won. The quote in this book is from Letter 419, to William Plomer, December 12, 1957, *Selected Letters*, published 1985.

AUGUST 1: **FRANK HERBERT** (10/8/1920–2/11/1986) was an American science fiction writer and the author of *Dune* and its numerous sequels. *Dune*, which is considered to be the world's bestselling science fiction saga, tells the story of the Atreides family, who live on a desert planet called Arrakis. The quote in this book is from *Dune*, 1965.

AUGUST 2: **LOUISA MAY ALCOTT** (11/29/1832–3/6/1888) was an American writer who grew up in a family that was very much part of the Transcendentalist philosophical movement in New England. Emerson, Thoreau, and Hawthorne were friends of her family, and Louisa grew up yearning to be a writer and make a name for herself, much like her protagonist Jo March in her most well-known and beloved novel, *Little Women*. Alcott also wrote the sequels to *Little Women*—*Little Men* and *Jo's Boys*—as well as numerous other works of fiction.

AUGUST 3: **NORMAN COUSINS** (6/24/1915–11/30/1990) was a journalist, literary critic, and liberal activist. He worked for the *New York Evening Post* and the *Saturday Review of Literature*. In 1964, at the age of forty-nine, he was told he had a fatal illness and only a short time to live. He combated the illness unconventionally—by taking massive doses of vitamin C and dedicating his time to watching Marx Brothers films—and lived another twenty-six years.

AUGUST 4: **ALFRED, LORD TENNYSON** (8/6/1809–10/6/1892) was poet laureate of Great Britain and Ireland during the time of Queen Victoria. Several phrases from his work remain in the English language today, for example: "'Tis better to have loved and lost / Than never to have loved at all."

AUGUST 5: **MATSUO BASHŌ** (1644–1694) was one of the most celebrated Japanese poets of all time. He began writing as a child and eventually renounced his ordinary life to find inspiration for his poetry in the wilderness. Today, he is considered to be the greatest master of the haiku poetry form.

AUGUST 6: **MARY ANNE RADMACHER** (present) is an artist and a writer of inspirational books. She has written ten books, including *Lean Forward into Your Life*, *Live with Intention*, and *Life Begins When You Do*.

AUGUST 7: See **ALICE WALKER**, February 6

AUGUST 8: **ANDRÉ GIDE** (11/22/1869–2/19/1951) was a French author and essayist who is best known for his work *Les faux-monnayeurs (The Counterfeiters)*. He was honored with the Nobel Prize in Literature in 1947. The quote in this book is from *Les faux-monnayeurs (The Counterfeiters)*, 1925.

AUGUST 9: **A. C. FIFIELD** (early 1900s) was the founder of a British publishing house called A. C. Fifield, which is credited with having published H. G. Wells and Samuel Butler.

AUGUST 10: **DOUG FLOYD** (present) is a communication specialist and motivational speaker who encourages groups and individuals to reach their maximum potential through clear communication.

AUGUST 11: **E. B. (ELWYN BROOKS) WHITE** (7/11/1899–10/1/1985) was an American author best remembered for his beloved children's books *Charlotte's Web* and *Stuart Little*. White was also coauthor of the classic English-language style guide *The Elements of Style*.

AUGUST 12: **GEORGE BERNARD SHAW** (7/26/1856–11/2/1950) was an Irish playwright and author of more than sixty plays. *Pygmalion*, his most famous play, earned him an Academy Award for his film adaptation. Shaw was an ardent opponent of inequality among social classes and supported socialism. The quote on this date is from *Back to Methuselah*, 1921.

AUGUST 13: **JANA STANFIELD** (present) is a musician and motivational speaker. She has written songs for Reba McEntire, Andy Williams, Kenny Loggins, and John Schneider, and has toured the country lecturing and singing her unique brand of inspirational music.

AUGUST 15: **GAIUS SALLUSTIUS CRISPUS** (86–35 BC), generally known as Sallust, was a Roman politician and historian whose works provided future historians with insight into the events of his era.

AUGUST 16: **BALTASAR GRACIÁN** (1/8/1601–12/6/1658) was a Spanish philosopher and writer, as well as a Jesuit priest. He taught in various Jesuit schools and became famous for his dramatic preaching. He is best known for *Criticón (Faultfinder)*, an allegorical novel about the conflict between disillusionment and innocence.

AUGUST 17: See **A. A. MILNE**, January 19

AUGUST 18: **JOSEPH JOUBERT** (5/7/1754–5/4/1824) was a French writer who didn't actually publish anything during his lifetime. His journals, in which he recorded his reflections on a broad range of topics, were published posthumously by Chateaubriand in 1838.

AUGUST 19: See **NELSON MANDELA**, February 19

AUGUST 20: **BRUCE LEE** (11/27/1940–7/20/1973) was an American-born Chinese martial artist who produced and starred in five martial arts films, including *Enter the Dragon* and *Fist of Fury*.

AUGUST 23: **PHILIP DORMER STANHOPE** (9/22/1694–3/24/1773), the 4th Earl of Chesterfield, was a British statesman. His thirty-year correspondence with his son Philip, on a range of subjects from manners to achieving success, was published in 1774 as *Letters to His Son on the Art of Becoming a Man of the World and a Gentleman*. The quote in this book is from a letter to his son on March 10, 1746.

AUGUST 24: See **JOHN DONNE**, January 4

AUGUST 28: See **RABINDRANATH TAGORE**, June 19

AUGUST 30: See **MARCUS AURELIUS**, May 23

AUGUST 31: See **ALFRED, LORD TENNYSON**, August 4

SEPTEMBER 1: **DR. WAYNE W. DYER** (5/10/1940–present) is a motivational speaker and author of over forty books, including the bestsellers *10 Secrets for Success and Inner Peace* and *The Power of Intention*. The quote in this book is from a blog post, "Letting Go," April 2010.

SEPTEMBER 2: **QUINTUS HORATIUS FLACCUS** (12/8/65–11/27/8 BC), known as Horace, lived during the reign of Augustus and was one of the most celebrated poets of his day. His works, which expounded on everyday subjects and revealed his Epicurean leanings, influenced many poets after him, including Ben Jonson and Robert Frost.

SEPTEMBER 3: **EURIPIDES** (484–406 BC) was a Greek playwright known for his tragic plays, particularly *Medea*, *The Trojan Women*, and *Iphigenia at Aulis*.

SEPTEMBER 4: See **GEORGE BERNARD SHAW**, August 12

SEPTEMBER 5: See **KAHLIL GIBRAN**, January 9

SEPTEMBER 6: See **DANTE ALIGHIERI**, February 9

SEPTEMBER 9: See **FATHER FABER**, May 4

SEPTEMBER 10: **FREDERICK DOUGLASS** (February 1818–2/20/1895) was an author and preacher whose life and work inspired the abolitionist movement in nineteenth-century America. He was born into slavery, from which he escaped. Later, his lectures and antislavery writing—specifically his autobiography *Narrative of the Life of Frederick Douglass, an American Slave*—shattered people's negative stereotypes about slaves. The book became a bestseller. Douglass was also a supporter of women's rights and was the first African American nominated for vice president of the United States. Quoted in this book from an address on West India Emancipation, August 3, 1857.

SEPTEMBER 11: See **WALT WHITMAN**, March 3

SEPTEMBER 12: **BELLA ABZUG** (7/24/1920–3/31/1998) was a women's rights activist and a U.S. congresswoman. She cofounded the National Women's Political Caucus and the Women's Environment and Development Organization, which promotes human rights around the world.

SEPTEMBER 14: **TAVIS SMILEY** (9/13/1964–present) is an American author and television personality. He was an aide to Tom Bradley, the mayor of Los Angeles in the 1980s, and later went on to host *The Tavis Smiley Show* on NPR from 2002 to 2004. In 2004 he became host of the television show *Tavis Smiley* on PBS, as well as the radio show *The Tavis Smiley Show* on Public Radio International.

SEPTEMBER 15: **KEN VENTURI** (5/15/1931–5/17/2013) was a professional American golfer and a sports commentator on network television. He first gained recognition in 1956 when, as an amateur, he finished second in the Masters Tournament.

SEPTEMBER 17: **ARISTOTLE** (384–322 BC) was a Greek philosopher who studied under Plato in Athens. A writer as well as a teacher, Aristotle covered a variety of subjects in his vast works—consisting mostly of notes and dialogues—from scientific annotations to poetry to ethics to how to live a good life. He is considered one of the first and greatest philosophers and scientists in history.

SEPTEMBER 18: **THEODOR SEUSS GEISEL** (3/2/1904–9/24/1991), or Dr. Seuss, was an American children's book author and illustrator, most remembered for his classic picture books *The Cat in the Hat, Green Eggs and Ham, The Lorax, Horton Hears a Who!,* and *How the Grinch Stole Christmas!*

SEPTEMBER 19: **SIR ARTHUR CONAN DOYLE** (5/22/1859–7/7/1930) was a Scottish writer best known for his Sherlock Holmes series, about a fictional detective named Sherlock and his partner, Dr. John H. Watson. This series is one of the most influential in the field of crime fiction. Conan Doyle also wrote plays, romances, nonfiction, historical novels, and science fiction books. The quote in this book is from *The Hound of the Baskervilles*, 1902.

SEPTEMBER 20: See **HELEN KELLER**, May 13

SEPTEMBER 21: **MICHAEL P. WATSON** (present) is a real estate investor, author, and speaker. He is best known for his book *The "Highest and Best" Real Estate Investment: How to Make Million Dollar Profits in the 21st Century.* He also leads various workshops to teach his personal techniques and methodologies that are focused on getting the most out of one's property investments.

SEPTEMBER 22: See **HENRY DAVID THOREAU**, April 8

SEPTEMBER 23: **MARTIN LUTHER KING, JR.** (1/15/1929–4/4/1968) was an American civil rights leader in the 1950s and 1960s who used nonviolent protest to promote equal rights for black people in the United States. In 1963, he led a March on Washington, which is where he delivered his famous "I Have a Dream" speech. He was awarded the Nobel Peace Prize in 1964, four years before his assassination at the age thirty-nine. Martin Luther King Jr. Day, the third Monday of January every year, is a national holiday in memory of his life and work. The quotes in this book are from his Nobel Peace Prize acceptance speech, December 10, 1964 (September 23); and from his "The Rising Tide of Racial Consciousness" address at the Golden Anniversary Conference of the National Urban League, September 6, 1960.

SEPTEMBER 25: **CARL SANDBURG** (1/6/1878–7/22/1967) was a major American writer and poet. He won Pulitzer Prizes for both of his collections of poems, *The Complete Poems of Carl Sandburg* and *Corn Huskers,* and also for his biography of Abraham Lincoln, *Abraham Lincoln: The War Years.* He was referred to as "the voice of America" by President Lyndon B. Johnson. The quote in this book is from *Slabs of the Sunburnt West,* 1922.

SEPTEMBER 27: **WILLIAM WORDSWORTH** (4/7/1770–4/23/1850) was one of the most important English poets of the Romantic Age. He was Britain's poet laureate from 1843 until his death in 1850. His best-known work is *The Prelude,* which was published after his death.

SEPTEMBER 28: **JAMES VILA BLAKE** (1/21/1842–4/28/1925) was an American minister and writer who served as pastor of several churches in Massachusetts and Illinois. His book *More Than Kin: A Book of Kindness* is still in print. In addition to his poetry, Blake wrote the words for many hymns that are still sung today. The quote in this book is from *More Than Kin: A Book of Kindness,* 1893.

SEPTEMBER 30: **HENRI MATISSE** (12/31/1869–11/3/1954) was a French artist who, along with Pablo Picasso and Marcel Duchamp, is considered a key founder of the modern art movement. His famous painting *The Dance*, which depicts a ring of dancers against a blue background, is one of the most recognized works of art in the world today.

OCTOBER 2: **G. K. (GILBERT KEITH) CHESTERTON** (5/29/1874–6/14/1936) was an English writer best known for his Father Brown books, which are about a parish priest who uses his intuition and understanding of the human soul to solve crimes. Chesterton himself was a fervent Catholic and believed in the economic ideology of distributism. The quote in this book is from *Illustrated London News*, April 29, 1922.

OCTOBER 5: See **THEODOR SEUSS GEISEL**, September 18

OCTOBER 7: **SALLY KOCH** (present) is a humanitarian affiliated with the Jesuit Volunteer Corps.

OCTOBER 8: See **AUSTIN KLEON**, April 29

OCTOBER 9: See **JOHANN WOLFGANG VON GOETHE**, March 27

OCTOBER 10: **AMY TAN** (2/19/1952–present) is a Chinese American writer best known for *The Joy Luck Club*, which was made into a film in 1993 and has been translated into thirty-five languages. She has written several other bestselling novels, such as *The Kitchen God's Wife*, *The Hundred Secret Senses*, *The Bonesetter's Daughter*, and *Saving Fish from Drowning*. She is also the author of two children's books, *The Moon Lady* and *The Chinese Siamese Cat*.

OCTOBER 11: **JOHN BURROUGHS** (4/3/1837–3/29/1921) was an American nature writer and early advocate of the conservation movement in the United States.

OCTOBER 12: See **FATHER FABER**, May 4

OCTOBER 15: See **VOLTAIRE**, March 15

OCTOBER 16: See **VICTOR HUGO**, January 29

OCTOBER 19: **HARRY STYLES** (2/1/1994–present) is a British singer in the popular band One Direction. He made his first television appearance as a solo contestant on the British talent show *The X Factor*. After being eliminated as a soloist, he was brought back into the competition with four other contestants to form the group that became One Direction. Since skyrocketing to fame, he has also appeared on television and in films.

OCTOBER 20: **PINDAR** (522–443 BC) was an ancient Greek poet, most famous for his choral odes in honor of notable people. He is widely considered to be the greatest lyric poet of his day, which may be one of the reasons many of his works have survived.

OCTOBER 21: See **CARL SAGAN**, January 8

OCTOBER 23: **IAN MACLAREN** (11/3/1850–5/6/1907) is the pen name of Rev. John Watson, a Scottish author and theologian. He is best known for his popular books *Beside the Bonnie Brier Bush* and *The Days of Auld Lang Syne*. There is some controversy about the origin of the quote attributed to him "Be kind, for everyone you meet is fighting a hard battle": it is sometimes misattributed to Plato, but the quote seems to be taken from Maclaren's "Be pitiful, for every man is fighting a hard battle."

OCTOBER 24: See **VICTOR HUGO**, January 29

OCTOBER 25: See **HELEN KELLER**, May 13

OCTOBER 26: **ANTOINE DE SAINT EXUPÉRY** (6/29/1900–7/31/1944) was a French author and aviator who is best known for his novella *Le petit prince* (*The Little Prince*), which has been translated into over 250 languages. He won several distinguished literary awards in France and was honored with the National Book Award in the United States. His plane vanished on a reconnaissance mission in 1944 while working for the Free French Air Force in North Africa during World War II. The quote in this book is from *Le petit prince* (*The Little Prince*), 1943.

OCTOBER 27: **MORRIS MANDEL** (1911–2009) was an American author and educator who wrote advice columns for the *Jewish Press* for almost fifty years.

OCTOBER 29: See **ALBERT SCHWEITZER**, April 23

OCTOBER 30: **KATY PERRY** (10/25/1984–present), born Katheryn Elizabeth Hudson, is an American pop singer and songwriter. She first became famous for her song "I Kissed a Girl," as well as other chart-topping singles, like "California Gurls," "Teenage Dream," and "Firework." Her third album was the first by a female recording artist to yield five number one songs on the *Billboard* chart. She is also a UNICEF Goodwill Ambassador and devotes time to other charitable organizations.

OCTOBER 31: **HUGH BLACK** (3/26/1868–4/6/1953) was a Scottish author of several books and sermons, including *Friendship, Culture and Restraint, Christ's Service of Love, The New World, The Adventure of Being Man,* and *Christ or Caesar.*

NOVEMBER 1: See **CONFUCIUS**, March 9

NOVEMBER 2: See **SENECA**, January 27

NOVEMBER 4: **OPRAH WINFREY** (1/29/1954–present) is an American philanthropist, media personality, author, and actress, best known for her talk show *The Oprah Winfrey Show,* which won numerous awards and was the highest-rated program of its kind in history. Although she was born into poverty, she is now a billionaire, devoting much of her fortune and time to charitable works, including the founding of the Oprah Winfrey Leadership Academy for Girls in South Africa.

NOVEMBER 5: **ERNESTO SÁBATO** (6/24/1911–4/30/2011) was an Argentinean writer. Trained as a physicist, he began writing essays and literary criticisms before turning his hand to novels. His first, *El Túnel,* was a psychological novel about a painter. He was honored for his writing with the Cervantes Prize in 1984, and he is considered to be one of the most influential writers in Argentine literature.

NOVEMBER 6: **HUGH PRATHER** (1/23/1938–11/15/2010) was an American author known for his bestselling book, *Notes to Myself: My Struggle to Become a Person,* which began as his journal.

NOVEMBER 9: **MILTON BERLE** (7/12/1908–3/27/2002) was an American comedian and actor. He hosted the *Texas Star Theater* comedy-variety show through the 1950s, and later starred in numerous film and television productions, including *It's a Mad, Mad, Mad, Mad World.*

NOVEMBER 10: See **MARCUS AURELIUS**, May 23

NOVEMBER 11: See **DALAI LAMA,** March 10

NOVEMBER 12: **DODINSKY** (present) is the author of the *New York Times* bestseller *In the Garden of Thoughts,* which started as a blog. Dodinsky writes about compassion, tolerance, and love.

NOVEMBER 13: **ROBERT BRAULT** (1963–present) is an American motivational author of short observations and words of wisdom. His works have appeared in magazines and newspapers for over forty years. He is the author of *Round Up the Usual Subjects: Thoughts on Just About Everything.* The quote in this book is from a blog post, November 2009.

NOVEMBER 14: **TAYLOR SWIFT** (12/13/1989–present) is an American singer and songwriter, and winner of seven Grammy awards. She is the youngest artist in music industry history to win Album of the Year. She has a large worldwide following of fans who identify with her catchy, personal songs, which transcend different genres. The quote in this book is from an interview in *Seventeen* magazine, June 2008.

NOVEMBER 15: See **HARRY STYLES,** October 19

NOVEMBER 16: **REBA McENTIRE** (3/28/1955–present) is an American country music singer and songwriter. She has won numerous recording industry awards, including two Grammys and fourteen American Music Awards, and she is widely recognized as the biggest female hit maker in country music history. She is also a television, film, and Broadway star. The quote in this book is from *Reba: My Story,* 1995.

NOVEMBER 17: **MARY BAKER EDDY** (7/16/1821–12/3/1910) was the founder of the controversial religious movement called Christian Science, which believes in the power of prayer as the best (and sometimes sole) recourse for combating physical ailments.

NOVEMBER 18: **STEVE MARABOLI** (present) is a motivational speaker and author. He is the founder of the philanthropic organization called A Better Today International, which has humanitarian programs in over forty countries.

NOVEMBER 19: **SAMUEL TAYLOR COLERIDGE** (10/21/1772–7/25/1834) was a British poet and one of the founders of the Romantic movement in England. He is best known for his poem "The Rime of the Ancient Mariner."

NOVEMBER 21: **ALAIN BOUBLIL** (3/5/1941–present) wrote the libretto and lyrics for the French musical *Les Misérables*, a play based on the novel by Victor Hugo about the struggles of Jean Valjean against an oppressive social system in post-revolutionary France. The musical's London production has never closed since its October 1985 opening. The quote in this book is from "Epilogue" in *Les Misérables, The Musical*, 1980.

NOVEMBER 22: **ERIC HOFFER** (7/25/1902–5/21/1983) was an American philosopher and author best known for his book *The True Believer*, in which he analyzed the similarity between the rise of all cultural and political mass movements. Hailing from a working-class family in the Bronx, Hoffer lost his eyesight when he was seven, then gained it back at the age of fifteen. Fearing he might lose it again, he became a voracious reader. The quote in this book is from *The Passionate State of Mind and Other Aphorisms*, 1955.

NOVEMBER 23: **CLEVELAND AMORY** (9/2/1917–10/14/1998) was an American author, television personality, and champion of animal rights. He founded the Black Beauty Ranch in 1979, a refuge for more than a thousand rescued animals—wild and domestic—who might otherwise have been abused or slaughtered.

NOVEMBER 24: **MARCEL PROUST** (7/10/1871–11/18/1922) was a French novelist whose masterwork, *À la recherche du temps perdu*, which is usually translated as *Rembrance of Things Past*, is considered to be one of the greatest French masterpieces of all time.

NOVEMBER 25: **HENRY WADSWORTH LONGFELLOW** (2/27/1807–3/24/1882) was an American poet, teacher, and abolitionist who is noted as being the first American to translate Dante's *The Divine Comedy*. His best-known works include *The Song of Hiawatha*, *Evangeline*, and "Paul Revere's Ride." The quote in this book is from "The Arrow and the Song," 1845.

NOVEMBER 28: **BEVERLY SILLS** (5/25/1929–7/2/2007), an opera singer whose career lasted more than forty years, helped popularize opera in the United States. After retiring in 1980, she went on to manage the New York City Opera and became chairwoman of Lincoln Center and, later, the Metropolitan Opera.

NOVEMBER 30: **CHRISTOPHER MORLEY** (5/5/1890–3/28/1957) was an American author of more than a hundred novels, essays, and volumes of poetry. His works include *Kitty Foyle*, *Thunder on the Left*, and *Parnassus* *on Wheels*. He was a contributing editor to the *Saturday Review of Literature*, the *New York Evening Post*, and other anthologies and literature reviews.

DECEMBER 1: **VIRGIL** (10/15/70–9/21/19 BC) was a Roman poet during the reign of Augustus. Virgil's epic work, *The Aeneid*, is one of the masterpieces of world literature. The poem tells the story of the escape of Aeneas during the fall of Troy and his arrival in Italy, and the eventual founding of Rome. The quote in this book is from *Aeneid*, Book X, (30–19 BC).

DECEMBER 2: See **MARCEL PROUST**, November 24

DECEMBER 4: See **LOUISA MAY ALCOTT**, August 2

DECEMBER 5: See **WILLIAM WORDSWORTH**, September 27

DECEMBER 6: **CHARLES SPURGEON** (6/19/1834–1/31/1892) was a British author and preacher known for his fiery and eloquent sermons. Having started his career at a small Baptist church, he began preaching in London, where, eventually, he would appear before crowds of over ten thousand people at a time.

DECEMBER 7: See **THOMAS JEFFERSON**, February 26

DECEMBER 10: See **HENRY WARD BEECHER**, July 7

DECEMBER 11: **WALT DISNEY** (12/5/1901–12/15/1966) was an American film producer and the founder, along with his brother, of the Walt Disney Company. He and his staff created many of the most beloved and beautiful animated films of all time, including *Snow White and the Seven Dwarfs*, *Pinocchio*, *Bambi*, *The Lion King*, *Lady and the Tramp*, and *Fantasia*, as well as iconic characters such as Mickey Mouse, Donald Duck, and Cruella de Vil. He was the recipient of twenty-two Academy Awards and seven Emmy Awards.

DECEMBER 12: See **MARTIN LUTHER KING, JR.**, September 23

DECEMBER 13: See **C. S. LEWIS**, May 8

DECEMBER 14: **CHARLES M.** Schulz (11/26/1922–2/12/2000) was an American cartoonist best known for his comic strip *Peanuts*, which features the characters Charlie Brown, his dog Snoopy, and friends Lucy, Linus, Schroeder, Peppermint Patty, and Pig-Pen, among others. *Peanuts* was published in seventy-five countries and in 2,600 daily newspapers for nearly fifty years. He is still considered to be one of the most influential cartoonists of all time.

DECEMBER 16: **AUDREY HEPBURN** (5/4/1929–1/20/1993) was an actress who first came to fame in the role of Princess Ann in *Roman Holiday,* for which she won an Oscar, a Golden Globe, and a BAFTA Award—the first actor in history to win all three for a single performance. She also starred in several other successful films, like *Sabrina, Breakfast at Tiffany's,* and *My Fair Lady,* which propelled her to even greater fame. Hepburn eventually left acting to pursue charitable work, traveling to underserved communities throughout the world to help impoverished children, and became the UNICEF International Goodwill Ambassador. She was awarded the Presidential Medal of Freedom in 1992 in recognition of her tireless work on behalf of others.

DECEMBER 18: **MAYA ANGELOU** (4/4/1928–5/28/2014) was an American author and civil rights activist. She is best known for her book *I Know Why the Caged Bird Sings,* which is now taught in colleges around the world. She was nominated for the Pulitzer Prize for her poetry collection *Just Give Me a Cool Drink of Water 'fore I Diiie.* The quote in this book is from *I Know Why the Caged Bird Sings,* 1969.

DECEMBER 19: See **J.R.R. TOLKIEN**, January 17

DECEMBER 20: See **MAHATMA GANDHI**, April 6

DECEMBER 22: **DESMOND TUTU** (10/7/1931–present) is a South African social rights activist, author, and crusader against apartheid. As the first black archbishop of Capetown, he used his fame to campaign for equal rights and called for the economic boycott of South Africa by other nations. He won the Nobel Peace Prize in 1984, and although retired from public life since 2010, he continues to work on behalf of humanitarian causes around the world.

DECEMBER 23: **DEMOCRITUS** (460–370 BC) was a Greek philosopher who is best known for formulating the atomic theory of the cosmos. He postulated that all things are made of combinations of invisible, indivisible, tiny particles, which he called atoms. This was two thousand years before modern atomic theory became a precise mathematical science with the advent of quantum mechanics.

DECEMBER 24: **ATHENAEUS** (c. AD 200) was a Greek author best known for his fifteen-volume *Deipnosophistai* (*The Dinner-Table Philosophers*), which is about a group of learned men discussing a variety of subjects, including food. This book was particularly useful to scholars because it contains references to nearly eight hundred other works of the time, which would otherwise have been lost.

DECEMBER 25: See **ST. FRANCIS OF ASSISI**, June 3

DECEMBER 26: **GAMALIEL BAILEY** (12/3/1807–6/5/1859) was an American journalist and publisher and a leader of the abolitionist movement. He is best known for publishing Harriet Beecher Stowe's influential novel *Uncle Tom's Cabin* in serial form in the *National Era* daily newspaper, which moved a great number of people to adopt anti-slavery views.

DECEMBER 29: **BERNARD BARUCH** (8/19/1870–6/20/1965) was an American financier and economic adviser to six presidents, most notably to Presidents Woodrow Wilson and Franklin D. Roosevelt, during both world wars.

DECEMBER 30: **NOEL CLARASÓ** (12/3/1899–1/18/1985) was a Spanish writer and dramatist who wrote numerous works on a great variety of subjects, from psychological thrillers to gardening books. Throughout his work, he was known for his humor.

DECEMBER 31: See **MOTHER TERESA**, March 20

CONTRIBUTORS OF ORIGINAL PRECEPTS, ARTWORK, AND LETTERING

JANUARY 2: Roald Dahl quote contributed by Nate, age 10, Brooklyn, N.Y.

JANUARY 11: Paul Brandt quote contributed by Elia, age 13, Regina, Sask., Canada.

JANUARY 26: Oscar Wilde quote contributed by Faith, Greensboro, N.C.

JANUARY 31: Original precept by Dominic, Bennington, Vt.

FEBRUARY 4: Original precept by Madison, age 11, Port Jefferson, N.Y.

FEBRUARY 7: Original precept by Emily, age 11, Port Jefferson Station, N.Y.

FEBRUARY 10: Original precept by Rebecca, age 10, Troy, Mich.

FEBRUARY 13: Original precept by Lindsay, age 11, Troy, Mich.

FEBRUARY 16: Lloyd Jones quote contributed by Liam, age 13, Regina, Sask., Canada.

FEBRUARY 17: Original precept by Jack, age 11, Hudson, Mass.

FEBRUARY 23: Original precept by Shreya, age 10, Troy, Mich.

MARCH 5: Original precept by Antonio, age 11, San Ramon, Calif. Art by Joseph Gordon.

MARCH 7: Ralph Waldo Emerson quote contributed by Linh, age 13, Regina, Sask., Canada.

MARCH 13: Henry Stanley Haskins quote contributed by Deacon, age 12, Regina, Sask., Canada.

MARCH 18: Original precept by Cate, age 10, Nashville, Tenn.

MARCH 19: Original precept by Isabelle, age 10, Washington, D.C.

MARCH 21: Original precept by Matthew, age 11, Lanoka Harbor, N.J.

MARCH 22: Original precept by Thomas, St. George, Utah.

MARCH 24: Chinese proverb contributed by Nathan, age 13, Regina, Sask., Canada.

MARCH 25: Original precept by Ella, Bay Village, Ohio.

MARCH 31: Original precept by Kyler, age 10, Merrick, N.Y.

APRIL 5: Original precept by Delaney, age 10, Lanoka Harbor, N.J.

APRIL 6: Mahatma Gandhi quote contributed by Rosemary, age 10, Nashville, Tenn.

APRIL 11: Vince Lombardi quote contributed by Zachary, age 13, Regina, Sask., Canada.

APRIL 13: Original precept by Rory, age 11, Chicago, Ill.

APRIL 16: Ziggy quote contributed by Kate, age 11, Chicago, Ill.

APRIL 17: Artwork by Matthew, age 11, Jackson Heights, N.Y.

APRIL 19: Original precept by Anna, age 10, Glenview, Ill.

MAY 5: Vince Lombardi quote contributed by Emma, age 10, Dresden, Ohio.

MAY 7: Original precept by Grace, age 12, Croton-on-Hudson, N.Y.

MAY 14: Original precept by Dustin, Bennington, Vt.

MAY 16: Original precept by Gavin, age 10, Wilmette, Ill.

MAY 21: Original precept by Srishti, age 10, Troy, Mich.

MAY 27: Original precept by Flynn, age 10, Bowdoinham, Me.

MAY 28: Original precept by Madeline, age 11, Quebec, Canada.

JUNE 4: Bob Marley quote contributed by Angelina, age 11, Jackson Heights, N.Y.

JUNE 16: Original precept by Clare, age 11, State College, Penn.

JUNE 17: Original precept by Josh, age 10, Troy, Mich.

JUNE 25: Original precept by Emma, age 11, Croton-on-Hudson, N.Y.

JUNE 26: Original precept by Paco, age 26, Brazil.

JUNE 30: Original precept by Caleb, age 17, Brooklyn, N.Y.

JULY 12: Unknown precept contributed by Julia, age 10, Troy, Mich.

JULY 15: Anthony Robbins quote contributed by Cole, age 14, Regina, Sask., Canada.

JULY 20: Original precept by Mae, age 11, Marblehead, Mass.

JULY 23: Original precept by Matea, age 12, Regina, Sask., Canada.

AUGUST 5: Artwork by Ashley, age 11, Jackson Heights, N.Y.

AUGUST 10: Doug Floyd quote contributed by Abby, age 10, Merrick, N.Y.

AUGUST 26: Original precept by Ava, age 11, Blackstone, Mass.

AUGUST 30: Artwork by Ali, age 11, Jackson Heights, N.Y.

SEPTEMBER 8: Unknown precept contributed by Samantha, age 13, Regina, Sask., Canada.

SEPTEMBER 13: Original precept by Zöe, Greensboro, N.C.

SEPTEMBER 16: Original precept by Alexis, age 10, Quebec, Canada.

SEPTEMBER 24: Proverb contributed by Tayler, age 10, Dresden, Ohio.

SEPTEMBER 26: Original precept by Riley, age 10, St. George, Utah.

SEPTEMBER 29: Original precept by Elizabeth, age 9, Nashville, Tenn.

OCTOBER 3: Original precept by John, age 10, West Windsor, N.J.

OCTOBER 5: Dr. Seuss quote contributed by Katherine, Greensboro, N.C.

OCTOBER 14: Original precept by Daniel, age 12, Munich, Germany.

OCTOBER 22: Unknown precept contributed by Nate, age 10, Brooklyn, N.Y.

NOVEMBER 3: Original precept by Clark, age 12, Regina, Sask., Canada.

NOVEMBER 8: Original precept by J.J., Scotch Plains, N.J.

NOVEMBER 14: Taylor Swift quote contributed by Nikki, age 17, East Brunswick, N.J.

NOVEMBER 20: Original precept by Hailey, age 11, Chicago, Ill.

NOVEMBER 21: *Les Misérables* quote contributed by Katherine, age 11, San Diego, Calif.

NOVEMBER 27: Original precept by Nicolas, age 10, State College, Penn.

NOVEMBER 29: Original precept by Joseph, age 9, Brooklyn, N.Y.

DECEMBER 8: Original precept by Hanz, age 13, Regina, Sask., Canada.

DECEMBER 9: Original precept by Mairead, age 11, Franklin, Mass.

DECEMBER 13: C. S. Lewis quote contributed by Chidiadi, age 12, Regina, Sask., Canada.

DECEMBER 14: Charles M. Schulz quote contributed by Dani, age 14, East Brunswick, N.J.

DECEMBER 15: Original precept by Brody, age 10, Forked River, N.J.

DECEMBER 21: Original precept by Ainsley, age 10, Lakeview, N.Y.

DECEMBER 27: Original precept by Christina, El Paso, Tex.

DECEMBER 31: Original artwork: fox by Kevin, age 11, Jackson Heights, N.Y.; duck by Prasansha, age 11, Jackson Heights, N.Y.

Special thanks to Nikki Martinez, Dani Martinez, and Joseph Gordon for their help with additional art.

NOTE ON SOURCES: Every possible measure has been taken to ensure that the quotes in this book are attributed to their original sources. However, over the centuries, old maxims have had a way of resurfacing with variations in wording or different translations. For this book, where a famous quote or saying is commonly attributed to a specific person without dispute, the most common attribution is used, even if its original source cannot be verified. Where a quote is occasionally disputed, the attribution is credited as "unknown."

ACKNOWLEDGMENTS

So many people had a hand in making this book. I'd like to, first and foremost, acknowledge the amazing contribution of the children who sent in their precepts—whether they ended up being included in this volume or not. There were over 1,200 submissions from people all over the world. The ones included in this volume are the ones I thought represented the spirit of Mr. Browne's precepts best. Precepts aren't just maxims or pretty quotes, after all—they are words to live by, to elevate the soul, that celebrate the goodness in people.

I'd also like to thank my husband, Russell, and our two sons, Caleb and Joseph, for helping me go through all the submissions, one by one, and for their wisdom, insight, support, and love in all matters. I couldn't do ANYTHING without you guys.

Thank you to Alyssa Eisner Henkin of Trident Media for being so incredible to work with on every level. Thank you to Erin Clarke, my WONDERful editor, Nancy Hinkel, Lauren Donovan, Judith Haut, Barbara Marcus, and the incredible team at Random House. A special thank-you to Janet Wygal, Diane João, and Artie Bennett for doing such an amazing job copyediting and helping me source so many of these quotes.

Thanks, as always, to the teachers and librarians who inspired me growing up, and who continue to inspire children every day. *You* are the real wonders of the world!

AN EXCERPT FROM

WONDER

Choose Kind

There was a lot of shuffling around when the bell rang and everybody got up to leave. I checked my schedule and it said my next class was English, room 321. I didn't stop to see if anyone else from my homeroom was going my way: I just zoomed out of the class and down the hall and sat down as far from the front as possible. The teacher, a really tall man with a yellow beard, was writing on the chalkboard.

Kids came in laughing and talking in little groups but I didn't look up. Basically, the same thing that happened in homeroom happened again: no one sat next to me except for Jack, who was joking around with some kids who weren't in our homeroom. I could tell Jack was the kind of kid other kids like. He had a lot of friends. He made people laugh.

When the second bell rang, everyone got quiet and the teacher turned around and faced us. He said his name was Mr. Browne, and then he started talking about what we would be doing this semester. At a certain point, somewhere between *A Wrinkle in Time* and *Shen of the Sea,* he noticed me but kept right on talking.

I was mostly doodling in my notebook while he talked, but every once in a while I would sneak a look at the other students. Charlotte was in this class. So were Julian and Henry. Miles wasn't.

Mr. Browne had written on the chalkboard in big block letters:

P-R-E-C-E-P-T!

"Okay, everybody write this down at the very top of the very first page in your English notebook."

As we did what he told us to do, he said: "Okay, so who can tell me what a precept is? Does anyone know?"

No one raised their hands.

Mr. Browne smiled, nodded, and turned around to write on the chalkboard again:

PRECEPTS = RULES ABOUT REALLY IMPORTANT THINGS!

"Like a motto?" someone called out.

"Like a motto!" said Mr. Browne, nodding as he continued writing on the board. "Like a famous quote. Like a line from a fortune cookie. Any saying or ground rule that can motivate you. Basically, a precept is anything that helps guide us when making decisions about really important things."

He wrote all that on the chalkboard and then turned around and faced us.

"So, what are some *really important* things?" he asked us.

A few kids raised their hands, and as he pointed at them, they gave their answers, which he wrote on the chalkboard in really, really sloppy handwriting:

RULES. SCHOOLWORK. HOMEWORK.

"What else?" he said as he wrote, not even turning around. "Just call things out!" He wrote everything everyone called out.

FAMILY. PARENTS. PETS.

One girl called out: "The environment!"

THE ENVIRONMENT,

he wrote on the chalkboard, and added:

OUR WORLD!

"Sharks, because they eat dead things in the ocean!" said one of the boys, a kid named Reid, and Mr. Browne wrote down

SHARKS.

"Bees!" "Seatbelts!" "Recycling!" "Friends!"

"Okay," said Mr. Browne, writing all those things down. He turned around when he finished writing to face us again. "But no one's named the most important thing of all."

We all looked at him, out of ideas.

"God?" said one kid, and I could tell that even though Mr. Browne wrote "God" down, that wasn't the answer he was looking for. Without saying anything else, he wrote down:

WHO WE ARE!

"Who we are," he said, underlining each word as he said it. "Who we are! Us! Right? What kind of people are we? What kind of person are you? Isn't that the most important thing of all? Isn't that the kind of question we should be asking ourselves all the time? "What kind of person am I?

"Did anyone happen to notice the plaque next to the door of this school? Anyone read what it says? Anyone?"

He looked around but no one knew the answer.

"It says: 'Know Thyself,'" he said, smiling and nodding. "And learning who you are is what you're here to do."

"I thought we were here to learn English," Jack cracked, which made everyone laugh.

"Oh yeah, and that, too!" Mr. Browne answered, which I thought was very cool of him. He turned around and wrote in big huge block letters that spread all the way across the chalkboard:

MR. BROWNE'S SEPTEMBER PRECEPT:

WHEN GIVEN THE CHOICE BETWEEN BEING RIGHT OR BEING KIND, CHOOSE KIND.

"Okay, so, everybody," he said, facing us again, "I want you to start a brand-new section in your notebooks and call it Mr. Browne's Precepts."

He kept talking as we did what he was telling us to do.

"Put today's date at the top of the first page. And from now on, at the beginning of every month, I'm going to write a new Mr. Browne precept on the chalkboard and you're going to write it down in your notebook. Then we're going to discuss that precept and what it means. And at the end of the month, you're going to write an essay about it, about what it means to you. So by the end of the year, you'll all have your own list of precepts to take away with you.

"Over the summer, I ask all my students to come up with their very own personal precept, write it on a postcard, and mail it to me from wherever you go on your summer vacation."

"People really do that?" said one girl whose name I didn't know.

"Oh yeah!" he answered, "people really do that. I've had students send me new precepts years after they've graduated from this school, actually. It's pretty amazing."

He paused and stroked his beard.

"But, anyway, next summer seems like a long way off, I know," he joked, which made us laugh. "So, everybody relax a bit while I take attendance, and then when we're finished with that, I'll start telling you about all the fun stuff we're going to be doing this year—in *English*." He pointed to Jack when he said this, which was also funny, so we all laughed at that.

As I wrote down Mr. Browne's September precept, I suddenly realized that I was going to like school. No matter what.